LUCY GORDON

Accidentally Expecting!

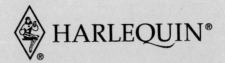

HARLEQUIN®

TORONTO • NEW YORK • LONDON
AMSTERDAM • PARIS • SYDNEY • HAMBURG
STOCKHOLM • ATHENS • TOKYO • MILAN • MADRID
PRAGUE • WARSAW • BUDAPEST • AUCKLAND

Recycling programs for this product may not exist in your area.

ISBN-13: 978-0-373-74010-9

ACCIDENTALLY EXPECTING!

First North American Publication 2010.

Copyright © 2009 by Lucy Gordon.

All rights reserved. Except for use in any review, the reproduction or utilization of this work in whole or in part in any form by any electronic, mechanical or other means, now known or hereafter invented, including xerography, photocopying and recording, or in any information storage or retrieval system, is forbidden without the written permission of the publisher, Harlequin Enterprises Limited, 225 Duncan Mill Road, Don Mills, Ontario, Canada M3B 3K9.

This is a work of fiction. Names, characters, places and incidents are either the product of the author's imagination or are used fictitiously, and any resemblance to actual persons, living or dead, business establishments, events or locales is entirely coincidental.

This edition published by arrangement with Harlequin Books S.A.

® and TM are trademarks of the publisher. Trademarks indicated with ® are registered in the United States Patent and Trademark Office, the Canadian Trade Marks Office and in other countries.

www.eHarlequin.com

Printed in U.S.A.

A special bonus from Lucy...
First Stop: Naples

I'll never forget my first view of Naples, a sunny, colorful place bristling with life and excitement, yet dominated by the presence of Vesuvius—silent, but one of the volcanoes in the world that can still erupt.

My hotel had six floors, and wise people take a room as high as possible because from there you get an uninterrupted view of the Bay of Naples, the glimmering lights around the shore, the moving lamps as the boats arrive and leave. And beyond, the endlessly patient, shadowy presence, waiting, not just today or tomorrow, but perhaps until the end of time.

On my first night I got up several times, to sit at the window and look out across the bay to the volcano that seemed to symbolize Naples itself: bright and cheery yet with a dark awareness that is never far away. The scenes where Dante and Ferne do the same came from that vivid experience.

Perhaps it was this intriguing dual character that originally made me choose Naples as the setting for my books about the Rinucci family, enabling me to come back again and again.

Of course, there is modern Naples, with fine upstanding buildings, industry and shipping, where fortunes can be made. But there are also the narrow streets where no car can go and there is room only for people, laughing, eating, bickering, loving.

A city where so many dramatic dark deeds have taken place is also where they invented the mandolin, useful for serenading a lady at night, and the pizza.

Next Stop: Falling in love…

My hero, Dante, wasn't born in Naples, but his spirit is Neapolitan—light and dark—forcing him to constantly juggle the balance. He lives for the moment, always ready for whatever comes next, swift, changeable, a willing lover, a generous friend, good-natured chancer.

To the casual eye he might seem shallow, laughing too much, loving too often, thinking too little. But nothing is quite as it seems, not Naples, not Dante. He's always been forced to conceal the truth that dominates his life, constricting his freedom and keeping him essentially apart from other people, so that, beneath the bonhomie he's the loneliest man in the world.

In this he's most truly a Neapolitan, for despite its lively exterior, this is a town of secrets, and the greatest secret of all is the existence of another Naples, underground. It was built five thousand years ago when the first inhabitants sheltered in grottoes carved out of sandstone, connected by narrow winding streets.

Today that place is deserted, save for tourists who descend to explore, but the next time you're in this glorious city, stop and look down. Just a few feet beneath you the first city is still there. And who knows? It will probably be there when the upper Naples is only a memory.

CHAPTER ONE

HORNS blared, lights flashed in the darkness and Ferne ground her hands together as the cab battled its way through the slow-moving Milan traffic.

'Oh no! I'm going to miss the train. *Please!*'

The driver called back over his shoulder, 'I'm doing my best, *signorina*, but the traffic here is like nowhere else in the world.' He said it with pride.

'I know it's not your fault,' she cried. 'But I've got a ticket on the night train to Naples. It leaves in a quarter of an hour.'

The driver chuckled. 'Leave it to me. Twenty years I am driving in Milan, and my passengers do not miss their trains.'

The next ten minutes were breathless but triumphant, and at last the ornate façade of Milan Central Station came into view. As Ferne leapt out and paid the driver, a porter appeared.

'Train to Naples,' she gasped.

'This way, *signorina*.'

They made it to the platform looking so frantic that heads were turned. But suddenly Ferne stumbled and went sprawling right in the path of the porter, who sprawled in turn.

She wanted to yell aloud at being thwarted at the last moment, but miraculously hands came out of nowhere, seized her, thrust her on board, the bags following after her. A door slammed.

'*Stai bene?*' came a man's voice.

'I'm sorry, I don't speak Italian,' she said breathlessly, clutching him as he helped her to her feet.

'I asked if you are all right,' he said in English.

'Yes, but—oh heavens, we're moving. I should have given that poor man something.'

'Leave it to me.'

There was a narrow opening at the top of the window and the man slid his arm through, his hand full of notes which the porter seized gratefully. Her rescuer waved and turned back to face her in the corridor of the train that was already gathering speed.

Now Ferne had a moment to look at him, and realised that she was suffering delusions. He was so handsome that it was impossible. In his thirties, he stood, tall and impressive, with wide shoulders and hair of a raven-black colour that only Italians seemed to achieve. His eyes were deep blue, gleaming with life, and his whole appearance was something no man could be permitted outside the pages of a novel.

To cap it all, he'd come galloping to her rescue like the hero of a melodrama, which was simply too much. But, what the heck? She was on holiday.

He returned her gaze, briefly but appreciatively, taking in her slender figure and dark-red hair. Without conceit, but also without false modesty, she knew she was attractive; the expression in his eyes was one she'd often seen before, although it was a while since she'd responded to it.

'I'll refund you that tip, of course,' she said.

A woman had appeared behind them in the corridor. She was in her sixties, white-haired, slender and elegant.

'Are you hurt, my dear?' she asked. 'That was a nasty fall you had.'

'No, I'm fine, just a bit shaken.'

'Dante, bring her to our compartment.'

'OK, Aunt Hope. You take her, I'll bring the bags.'

The woman took Ferne gently by the arm and led her along the corridor to a compartment where a man, also in his sixties, was standing in the doorway watching their approach. He stood back to let them in and ushered Ferne to a seat.

'From the way you speak, I think you are English,' the woman said with a charming smile.

'Yes, my name is Ferne Edmunds.'

'I too am English. At least, I was long ago. Now I am Signora Hope Rinucci. This is my husband, Toni—and this young man is our nephew, Dante Rinucci.'

Dante was just entering with the bags, which he shoved under the seats, and then he sat down, rubbing his upper arm.

'Are you hurt?' Hope asked anxiously.

He grimaced. 'Pushing my arm through that narrow space has probably left me with bruises for life.' Then a grin broke over his face. 'It's all right, I'm only joking. Stop fussing. It's our friend here who needs care. Those platforms are hard.'

'That's true,' Ferne said ruefully, rubbing her knees through her trousers.

'Would you like me to take a look?' he asked hopefully, reaching out a hand.

'No, she would not,' Hope said, determinedly forestalling him. 'Behave yourself. In fact, why don't you go to the restaurant-car and order something for this young lady?' She added sternly, 'Both of you.'

Like obedient little boys, both men rose and departed without a word. Hope chuckled.

'Now, *signorina*—it is *signorina*?'

'Signorina Edmunds. But, please, call me Ferne. After what your family has done for me, let's not be formal.'

'Good. In that case—'

There was a knock on the door and a steward looked in.

'Oh yes, you want to make up the berths,' Hope said. 'Let's join the men.'

As they went along the corridor, Hope asked, 'Where is your sleeping berth?'

'I don't have one,' Ferne admitted. 'I booked at the last minute and everything was taken.'

By now they had reached the dining-car, where Toni and Dante had taken a table. Dante stood up and graciously showed her to the seat beside him.

'Here's the ticket inspector,' Hope said. 'Let's get the formalities out of the way before we eat. They may be able to find you a berth.'

But from that moment things went horribly wrong. As the others showed their paperwork, Ferne scrabbled hopelessly in her bag, finally facing the terrible truth.

'It's gone,' she whispered. 'Everything. My money, the tickets—they must have fallen out when I fell on the platform.'

Another search produced no result. Disaster!

'My passport's gone too!' she gasped. 'I've got to go back.'

But the train was now travelling at full speed.

'It doesn't stop until Naples,' Hope explained.

'They'll stop to throw me off when they find out I've no ticket and no money,' Ferne said frantically.

Hope's voice was soothing. 'Let's see what we can do about that.'

Toni began to speak to the inspector in Italian. After a while he produced his credit card.

'They're issuing you another ticket,' Hope explained.

'Oh, that's so kind of you. I'll pay you back, I promise.'

'Let's not worry about that now. First we have to find you a berth.'

'That's easy,' Dante said. 'My sleeping-car is a double, and I'm only using one berth, so—'

'So Toni can come in with you and Ferne can come in with me,' Hope said, beaming. 'What a splendid idea!'

'Actually, Aunt, I was thinking—'

'I know what you were thinking and you should be ashamed.'

'Yes, Aunt, anything you say, Aunt.'

But he winked at Ferne, and she couldn't help being charmed. The mere idea of this handsome, confident man doing what he was told was so idiotic, and his air of meekness so clearly an act, that she had to smile and join in the joke.

The inspector exchanged some more words with Toni before nodding and hurrying away.

'He's going to call the station now and tell them to look out for your things,' Toni explained to Ferne. 'Luckily you discovered the loss quickly, so they may pick them up before anyone else finds them. But, just in case, you must cancel your credit cards.'

'How can I do that from here?' Ferne asked, baffled.

'The British consulate will help you,' Dante declared, taking out his own mobile phone.

In a few moments he had obtained the emergency number of the Milan consulate, dialled it and handed the phone to Ferne.

The young man on duty was efficient. Quickly he looked up the numbers of the credit-card companies, assigned her a reference number and bid her goodnight. Calls to the finance companies achieved the cancellation of her cards and the promise of new ones. This was as much as she could hope for for now.

'I don't know what I'd have done without you,' she told her new friends fervently. 'When I think what could have happened to me.'

'Don't think about it,' Hope advised. 'All will

be well. Ah, here is the waiter with a snack. Hmm, cakes and wine are all very well, but I should like a large pot of tea.'

'*English* tea.' Toni gave instructions to the waiter, who nodded solemnly, evidently familiar with this peculiarity among his customers.

The tea was excellent, so were the cakes, which the others piled onto her plate.

'When did you last eat?' Hope asked.

'Properly? Oh—some time. I left on the spur of the moment, caught the train from London to Paris, then Paris to Milan. I don't like flying, and I wanted to be free to stop and explore whenever I wanted. I had a few days in Milan, shopping and seeing the sights. I meant to stay there overnight and go on tomorrow, but I suddenly changed my mind, packed up and ran.'

'That's the way to live!' Dante exclaimed. 'Here today, gone tomorrow; let life bring what it will.' He took Ferne's hand and spoke with theatrical fervour. '*Signorina*, you are a woman after my own heart. More than a woman—a goddess with a unique understanding of life. I salute you—why are you laughing?'

'I'm sorry,' Ferne choked. 'I can't listen to that guff with a straight face.'

'Guff? *Guff?* Is this a new English word?'

'No,' Hope informed him, amused. 'It's an old

English word and it means that you need a better scriptwriter.'

'But only for me,' Ferne chuckled. 'I expect it works wonderfully on the others.'

Dante's face was the picture of outrage.

'The others? Don't you realise that you are the only one who has inspired me to lay my heart at her feet? The only— Oh, all right; I usually get a better reception than this.'

His collapse into realism made them all laugh.

'It's nice to meet a lady with such an adventurous approach to life,' he added. 'But I expect it's only while you're on holiday. You'll go back to England, your sedate nine-to-five life, and your sedate nine-to-five fiancé.'

'If I had a fiancé, what would I be doing here alone?' she demanded.

This made him pause, but only for a moment.

'He betrayed you,' he said dramatically. 'You are teaching him a lesson. When you return, he will be jealous, especially when he sees the compromising pictures of us together.'

'Oh, will he indeed? And where will these pictures come from?'

'It can be arranged. I know some good photographers.'

'I'll bet you don't know anyone better than me,' she riposted.

'You're a photographer?' Hope asked. 'A journalist?'

'No, I do theatrical work.' Some inexplicable instinct made her say to Dante, 'And he wasn't sedate. Anything but.'

He didn't reply in words, but his expression was wry and curious. So was the way he nodded.

'Let the poor girl eat in peace,' Hope admonished him.

She watched Ferne like a mother hen, finally declaring that it was time for bed. The four of them made their way back along the corridor and said goodnight. Ferne and Hope went into one sleeping car, Toni and Dante went on to the next.

As Ferne hung up the trousers she'd been wearing, a few coins fell out onto the floor.

'I'd forgotten I had some money in my pocket,' she said, holding them out.

'Three euros,' Hope observed. 'You wouldn't have got far with that.'

They sat down on the bed, contentedly sipping the tea they had brought with them.

'You said you were English,' Ferne recalled. 'And yet you speak as though you've been here for some time.'

'Over thirty years,' Hope told her.

'Do you have any children?'

'Six. All sons.'

She said it with an air of exasperated irony that made Ferne smile and say, 'Do you ever wish you had daughters?'

Hope chuckled. 'When you have six sons, you have no time to think of anything else. Besides, I have six daughters-in-law and seven grandchildren.

'When our last son married, a few months ago, Toni and I decided to go on our travels. Recently we've been in Milan to see some of his relatives. Toni was very close to his other brother, Taddeo, until he died a few years ago. Dante is Taddeo's elder son, and he's coming back to Naples with us for a visit. He's a bit of a madman, as you'll discover while you're staying with us.'

'I can't impose on you any further.'

'My dear, you have no money or passport. If you don't stay with us, just what are you going to do?'

'It just seems dreadful for you to be burdened with me.'

'But I shall love having you. We can talk about England. I love Italy, but I miss my own country, and you can tell me how things are there now.'

'Ah, that's different, if there's something I can do for you.'

'I look forward to you staying with us a long time. Now, I must get some sleep.'

She got into the lower bunk. Ferne climbed to

the top one, and in a few minutes there was peace and darkness.

Ferne lay listening to the hum of the train speed through the night, trying to get her bearings. It seemed such a short time since she'd made the impulsive decision to leave England. Now she was here, destitute, reliant on strangers.

While she was pondering the strange path her life had taken recently, the rhythm of the train overtook her and she fell asleep.

She awoke to find herself desperately thirsty, and remembered that the snack bar was open all night. Quietly she climbed down and groped around in the darkness for her robe.

The three euros she'd found would just be enough for a drink. Holding her breath and trying not to waken Hope, she crept out into the corridor and made her way to the dining-car.

She was in luck. The snack bar was still open, although the tables were deserted and the attendant was nodding off.

'I'll have a bottle of mineral water, please,' she said thankfully. 'Oh dear, four euros. Do you have a small one?'

'I'm afraid the last small bottle has gone,' the attendant said apologetically.

'Oh *no*!' It came out as a cry of frustration.

'Can I help?' asked a voice behind her.

She turned and saw Dante.

'I'm on the cadge for money,' she groaned. '*Again*! I'm desperate for something to drink.'

'Then let me buy you some champagne.'

'No, thank you, just some mineral water.'

'Champagne is better,' he said in the persuasive voice of a man about to embark on a flirtation.

'No, water is better when you're thirsty,' she said firmly.

'Then I can't persuade you?'

'No,' she said, getting cross. 'You can't persuade me. What you can do is step out of my way so that I can leave. Goodnight.'

'I apologise,' he said at once. 'Don't be angry with me, I'm just fooling.' To the bartender he added, 'Serve the lady whatever she wants, and I'll have a whisky.'

He slipped an arm about her, touching her lightly but firmly enough to prevent her escape, and guided her to a seat by the window. The barman approached and she seized the bottle of water, threw back her head and drank deeply.

'That's better,' she said at last, gasping slightly. 'I should be the one apologising. I'm in a rotten temper, but I shouldn't take it out on you.'

'You don't like being dependent on people?' he guessed.

'Begging,' she said in disgust.

'Not begging,' he corrected her gently. 'Letting your friends help you.'

'I'll pay every penny back,' she vowed.

'Hush! Now you're getting boring.'

Fearing that he might be right, she swigged some more water. It felt good.

'You seem to be having a very disorganised holiday,' he observed. 'Have you been planning it for long?'

'I didn't plan it at all, just hurled a few things into a bag and flounced off.'

'That sounds promising. You said you're a photographer...' He waited hopefully.

'I specialise in the theatre, and film stills. *He's* an actor, starring in a West End play. Or, at least, he *was* in a West End play until—'

'You can't stop there!' he protested. 'Just when it's getting interesting.'

'I was taking the pics. We had a thing going— and, well, I didn't expect eternal fidelity—but I did expect his full attention while we were together.'

'A reasonable desire,' her companion said solemnly.

'So I thought, but an actress in the play started flashing her eyes at him. I think she saw him chiefly as a career step-up—Oh, I don't know, though. To be fair, he's very handsome.'

'Well known?' Dante asked.

'Sandor Jayley.'

Dante's eyes widened.

'I saw one of his films on television the other day,' he said. 'He's supposed to be headed for even greater things.' He assumed a declamatory voice. 'The man whose embrace all women dream of—whose merest look—'

'Oh, shut up!' she said through laughter. 'I can't keep a straight face at that twaddle, which used to really annoy him.'

'He took it seriously?'

'Yes. Mind you, he has plenty going for him.'

'Looks, allure…?'

'Dazzling smile, more charm than was good for him—or for me. Just the usual stuff. Nothing, really.'

'Yes, it doesn't amount to much,' he agreed. 'You have to wonder why people make such a fuss about it.'

They nodded in solemn accord.

He yawned suddenly, turning so that he was half-sideways and could raise one foot onto the seat beside him; he rested an arm on it and leaned his head back. Ferne studied him a moment, noticing the relaxed grace of his tall, lean body. His shirt was open at the throat, enough to reveal part of his smooth chest; his black hair was slightly on the long side.

She had to admit that he had 'the usual stuff', with plenty to spare. His face was not only handsome but intriguing, with well-defined, angular features, dark, wicked eyes and a look of fierce, humorous intelligence.

Quirky, she thought, considering him with a professional gaze. Always about to do or say something unexpected. That was what she'd try to bring out if she were taking his photograph.

Suddenly he looked at her, and the gleaming look was intense.

'So, tell me about it,' he said.

'Where do I start?' She sighed. 'The beginning, when I was starry-eyed and stupid, or later, when he was shocked by my "unprincipled vulgarity"?'

Dante was immediately alert.

'Unprincipled and vulgar, hmm? That sounds interesting. Don't stop.'

'I met Tommy when I was hired to take the photographs for the play—'

'Tommy?'

'Sandor. His real name is Tommy Wiggs.'

'I can see why he changed it. But I want to know how you were unprincipled and vulgar.'

'You'll have to wait for that bit.'

'Spoilsport!'

'Where was I? Ah, yes, taking pictures for the play. Thinking back, I guess he set out to make me fall for him because he reckoned it would give an extra something to the photographs. So he took me to dinner and dazzled me.'

'And you were taken in by actorly charm?' Dante asked, frowning a little, as though he found it hard to believe.

'No, he was cleverer than that. He made a great play of switching off the actor and just being *himself*, as he put it, saying he wanted to use his real name because Sandor was for the masses. The man inside was *Tommy*.' Seeing his face, she said, 'Yes, it makes me feel a bit queasy too, but that night it was charming.

'The thing is, Tommy was made to be a film actor, not a stage actor. He's more impressive in close-up, and the closer you get the better he seems.'

'And he made sure you got very close?'

'Not that night,' she murmured, 'but eventually.'

She fell silent, remembering moments that had been sweet at the time but in retrospect felt ridiculous. How easily she'd fallen, and how glad she was to be out of it now. Yet there had been other times that she still remembered with pleasure, however mistakenly.

Dante watched her face, reading it without difficulty, and his eyes darkened. He raised a hand to summon the attendant, and when Ferne looked up she found Dante filling a glass of champagne for her.

'I felt you needed it after all,' he said.

'Yes,' she murmured. 'Maybe I do.'

'So what was the film actor doing in a play?' Dante asked.

'He felt that people didn't take him seriously.'

'Heaven help us! One of them. They make a career out of being eye candy but it's not enough. They want to be *respected*.'

'You've got him to a T,' Ferne chuckled. 'Are you sure you don't know him?'

'No, but I've met plenty like him. Some of the houses I sell belong to that kind of person—"full of themselves", I believe is the English expression.'

'That's it. Someone persuaded him that if he did a bit of Shakespeare everyone would be impressed, so he agreed to star in *Antony and Cleopatra*.'

'Playing Antony, the great lover?'

'Yes. But I think part of the attraction was the fact that Antony was an ancient Roman, so he had to wear little, short tunics that showed off his bare legs. He's got very good legs. He even made the costume department take the tunics up a couple of inches to show off his thighs.'

Dante choked with laughter.

'It was very much an edited version of the play because he couldn't remember all the long speeches,' Ferne recalled. 'Mind you, he made them shorten Cleopatra's speeches even more.'

'In case she took too much of the spotlight?' Dante hazarded a guess.

'Right. He wasn't going to have that. Not that it really mattered, because everyone was looking at his thighs.'

'I don't think you're exactly heartbroken,' Dante commanded, watching her intently.

'Certainly not,' she said quickly. 'It was ridiculous, really. Just showbusiness. Or life.'

'How do you mean?'

'It's all a performance of one kind or another. We each live by pretending something's true when we really know it isn't, or not true when we know it is.'

A strange look came into his eyes, as though her words carried a particular resonance. He seemed about to say something, but then backed off. She had the impression that a corner of the curtain to his mind had been raised, then dropped hastily.

So there was more to him than the charming clown, she thought. He presented that aspect to the world, but behind it was another man who hid himself away and kept everyone else out. Intrigued, she wondered how easy it would be to reach behind his defences.

The next moment he gave her the answer.

Seeing her watching him, he closed his eyes, shutting her out completely.

CHAPTER TWO

SUDDENLY he opened his eyes again, revealing that the tension had gone. The dark moment might never have been. His next words were spoken lightly.

'You're getting very philosophical.'

'Sorry,' she said.

'Were you talking about yourself when you said we each live by refusing to admit the truth?'

'Well, I suppose I really knew that another woman had her eye on him, and I ought to have realised that he'd give in to flattery, no matter what he'd said to me hours before. But it was still a bit of a shock when I went to meet him at the theatre after the performance and found them together.'

'What were they doing—or needn't I ask?'

'You needn't ask. They were right there on the stage, stretched out on Cleopatra's tomb, totally oblivious to anyone and anything. She was saying, "Oh, you really are Antony—a great hero!"'

'And I suppose they were—' Dante paused delicately '—in a state of undress?'

'Well, he still had his little tunic on. Mind you, that was almost the same thing.'

'So what did you do?' he asked, fascinated. 'You didn't creep away in tears. Not you. You went and thumped him.'

'Neither.' She paused for dramatic effect. 'I hardly dare tell you what I did.'

'Have we got to the bit where you're unprincipled and vulgar?' he asked hopefully.

'We have.'

'Don't keep me in suspense. Tell me.'

'Well, I take my camera everywhere…'

Dante's crack of laughter seemed to hit the ceiling and echo around the carriage, waking the barman from his doze.

'You *didn't*?'

'I did. They were wonderful pictures. I took as many as I could from as many different angles as possible.'

'And he didn't see you?'

'He had his back to me,' Ferne explained. 'Facing downwards.'

'Oh yes, naturally. But what about her?'

'She was facing up and she saw me, of course.

She loved it. Then I stormed off in a temper, went straight to the offices of a newspaper that specialised in that sort of thing and sold the lot.'

Awed, he stared at her. 'Just like that?'

'Just like that.'

His respect grew in leaps and bounds; a woman who reacted to her lover's betrayal not with tears and reproaches but with well-aimed revenge was a woman after his own heart.

What couldn't she do if she set her mind to it?

Would any man of sense want to get on her wrong side?

But her right side—that was a different matter!

'What happened?' he demanded, still fascinated.

'There were ructions, but not for long. The seats had been selling reasonably well, but after that it was standing-room only. *She* gave an interview about how irresistible he was, and he got offered a big, new film-part. So then he walked out on the show, which annoyed Josh, the director, until the understudy took over and got rave reviews. He was Josh's boyfriend, so everyone was happy.'

'Everyone except you. What did you get out of it?'

'The paper paid me a fortune. By that time I'd calmed down a bit and was wondering if I'd gone too far, but then the cheque arrived, and, well…'

'You've got to be realistic,' he suggested.

'Exactly. Mick—that's my agent—said some people wait a lifetime for a stroke of luck like mine. I've always wanted to see Italy, so I planned this trip. I had to wait a couple of months because suddenly I was much in demand. I'm not sure why.'

'Word had spread about your unusual skills,' he mused.

'Yes, that must be it. Anyway, I made a gap in my schedule, because I was determined to come here, chucked everything into a suitcase, jumped on the next train to Paris and from there I got the train to Milan.

'I spent a few days looking over the town, then suddenly decided to take off for Naples. It was late in the evening by then and a sensible person would have waited until morning. So I didn't.'

Dante nodded in sympathy. 'The joy of doing things on the spur of the moment! There's nothing like it.'

'I've always been an organised person, perhaps too organised. It felt wonderful to go a bit mad.' She gave a brief, self-mocking laugh. 'But I'm not very good at it, and I really messed up, didn't I?'

'Never mind. With practice, you'll improve.'

'Oh no! That was my one fling.'

'Nonsense, you're only a beginner. Let me introduce you to the joys of living as though every moment was your last.'

'Is that how you live?'

He didn't reply at first. He'd begun to lean forward across the table, looking directly into her face. Now he threw himself back again.

'Yes, it's how I live,' he said. 'It gives a spice and flavour to life that comes in no other way.'

She felt a momentary disturbance. It was inexplicable, except that there had been something in his voice that didn't fit their light-hearted conversation. Only a moment ago he'd shut her out, and something told her he might just do so again. They had drifted close to dangerous territory, which seemed to happen surprisingly easily with this man.

Again, she wondered just what lay in that forbidden place. Trying to coax him into revelation, she mused, 'Never to know what will happen next—I suppose I'm living proof that that can make life interesting. When I woke up this morning, I never pictured this.'

His smile was back. The moment had passed.

'How could you have imagined that you'd meet one of this country's heroes?' he demanded irrepressibly. 'A man so great that his head is on the coins.'

Enjoying her bemused look, he produced a

two-euro coin. The head, with its sharply defined nose, did indeed bear a faint resemblance to him.

'Of course!' she said. 'Dante Alighieri, your famous poet. Is that how you got your name?'

'Yes. My mother hoped that naming me after a great man might make me a great man too.'

'We all have our disappointments to bear,' Ferne said solemnly.

His eyes gleamed appreciation at her dig.

'Do you know much about Dante?' he asked.

'Not really. He lived in the late-thirteenth to early-fourteenth century, and he wrote a master-piece called *The Divine Comedy*, describing a journey through hell, purgatory and paradise.'

'You've read it? I'm impressed.'

'Only in an English translation, and I had to struggle to reach the end.' She chuckled. 'Hell and purgatory were so much more interesting than paradise.'

He nodded. 'Yes, I always thought paradise sounded insufferable. All that virtue.' He shuddered, then brightened. 'Luckily, it's the last place I'm likely to end up. Have some more champagne.'

'Just a little.'

A train thundered past them, going in the opposite direction. Watching the lights flicker on him as it went, Ferne thought that it wasn't hard to picture him as a master of the dark arts; he was engaging and more than a little risky, because he masked his true self with charm.

She'd guessed he was in his early thirties, but in this light she changed the estimate to late thirties. There was experience in his face, both good and bad.

'What are you thinking?' he asked.

'I was wondering what part of the other world you might have come from.'

'No doubt about it, the seventh terrace of purgatory,' he said, one eyebrow cocked to see if she understood.

She did. The seventh terrace was reserved for those who had over-indulged in the more pleasurable sins.

'That's just what I thought,' she murmured. 'But I didn't want to suggest it in case you were offended.'

His wry smile informed her that this was the last accusation that would ever offend him.

For a few minutes they sipped champagne in silence. Then he remarked, 'You'll be staying with us, of course?'

'As Hope says, I don't have any choice, for a few days at least.'

'Longer, much longer,' he said at once. 'Italian bureaucracy takes its time, but we'll try to make your stay a pleasant one.'

His meaning was unmistakeable. *Well, why not?* she thought. She was in the mood for a flirtation with a man who would take it as lightly as herself. He was attractive, interesting and they both knew the score.

'I'll look forward to it,' she said. 'Actually, Hope wants me to talk to her about England, and it's the least I can do for her.'

'Yes, she must feel a bit submerged by Italians,' Dante said. 'Mind you, she's always been one of us, and the whole family loves her. My parents died when I was fifteen, and she's been like a second mother to me ever since.'

'Do you live here?'

'No, I'm based in Milan, but I came south with them because I think there are business opportunities in the Naples area. So after looking around I might decide to stay.'

'What do you do?'

'I deal in property, specialising in unusual places, old houses that are difficult to sell.'

He yawned and they sat together in companionable silence. She felt drained and contented at the same time, separated from the whole universe on this train, thundering through the night.

Looking up, she saw that he was staring out into the darkness. She could see his reflection faintly in the window. His eyes were open and held a faraway expression, as though he could see something in the gloom that was hidden from her and which filled him with a melancholy intensity.

He looked back at her and smiled, rising reluctantly to his feet and holding out his hand. 'Let's go.'

At the door to her carriage, he paused and said gently, 'Don't worry about anything. I promise you, it's all going to work out. Goodnight.'

Ferne slipped into the carriage, moving quietly so as not to waken Hope, who was asleep. In a moment she'd skimmed up the ladder and settled down in bed, staring into the night, wondering about the man she'd just left. He was likeable in a mad sort of way, and she didn't mind spending some time in his company, as long as it was strictly casual.

But she didn't brood. The rocking of the train was hypnotic, and she was soon asleep.

Next morning there was just time for a quick snack before they arrived. Hope looked eagerly out of the window, wondering which of her sons would meet them.

'Justin's in England and Luke's in Rome,' she said. 'Carlo's in Sicily and won't be back for a couple of days. It'll be one of the other three.'

In the end three sons were waiting at the station, waving and cheering as the train pulled in. They embraced their parents exuberantly, clapped Dante on the shoulder and eyed Ferne with interest.

'These are Francesco, Ruggiero and Primo,' Toni explained. 'Don't try to sort them out just now. We'll do the introductions later.'

'Ferne has had a misfortune and will be staying with us until it's sorted out,' Hope said. 'Now, I'm longing to get home.'

There were two cars. Hope, Toni and Ferne rode in the first, driven by Francesco, while the other two brothers took Dante and the luggage in the second.

All the way home Hope looked eagerly out of the window, until at last she seized Ferne's arm and said, 'Look. That's the Villa Rinucci.'

Ferne followed her gaze up to the top of a hill, on which was perched a large villa facing out over Naples and the sea. She was entranced by the place; it was bathed in golden sun, and looked as though it contained both beauty and safety.

As they grew nearer she saw that the house was larger than she'd realised at first. Trees surrounded it, but the villa was on slightly higher ground, so that it seemed to be growing out of the trees. A plump woman, followed by two buxom young girls, came out to watch the cars arriving, all waving eagerly.

'That's Elena, my housekeeper,' Hope told Ferne. 'The two girls are her nieces who are working here for a couple of weeks, because there will be so many of us—and plenty of children, I'm glad to say. I called Elena while we were still on the train, to tell her you were coming and would need a room.'

The next moment they stopped, the door was pulled open and Ferne was being shown up the steps onto the wide terrace that surrounded the house, and then inside.

'Why don't you go up to your room at once?' Hope asked. 'Come down when you're ready and meet these villains I call my sons.'

'These villains' were smiling with pleasure at seeing their parents again and Ferne slipped away, understanding that they would want to be free of her for a while.

Her room was luxurious, with its own bathroom and a wide, comfortable-looking bed. Going to the window, she found she was at the front of the house, with a stunning view over the Bay of Naples. It was at its best just now, the water glittering in the morning sun, stretching away to the horizon, seeming to offer an infinity of pleasure and unknown delight.

Quickly she showered and changed into a dress of pale blue, cut on simple lines but fashionable. At least she would be able to hold her head up in elegant Italy.

She heard laughter from below, and looked out

of the window to where the Rinucci family were seated around a rustic wooden table under the trees, talking and laughing in a gentle manner that made a sudden warmth come over her heart.

Her own family life had been happy but sparse. She was an only child, born to parents who were themselves only-children. One set of grandparents had died early, the other had emigrated to Australia.

Now her father was dead and her mother had gone to live with her own parents in Australia. Ferne could have gone too, but had chosen to stay in London to pursue a promising career. So there was only herself to blame that she was lonely, that there had been nobody to lend a sympathetic ear when the crash had come with Sandor Jayley.

There had been friends, of course, nights out with the girls that she'd genuinely enjoyed. But they were career women like herself, less inclined to sympathise than congratulate her on the coup she'd pulled off. She'd always returned to an empty flat, the silence and the memories.

But something told her that the Villa Rinucci was never truly empty, and she was assailed by delight as she gazed down at the little gathering.

Hope looked up and waved, signalling for her to join them, and Ferne hurried eagerly down the stairs and out onto the terrace. As she approached the table the young men stood up with an old-fashioned courtesy that she found charming, and Dante stepped forward to take her hand and lead her forward. Hope rose and kissed her.

'This is the lady who joined us on the train and who will be staying with us for a while,' she said.

She began to introduce the young men—first Primo, stepson from her first marriage, then Ruggiero, one of her sons by Toni. Both men were tall and dark. Primo's face was slightly heavier, while Ruggiero's features had a mobility that reminded her slightly of his cousin, Dante.

Francesco had a brooding quality, as though his mind carried some burden. Like the other two, he greeted her warmly, but then said, 'I'd better go now, Mamma. I want to get home before Celia.'

'Doesn't she ever get suspicious about how often that happens?' Hope asked.

'Always, and she tells me to stop, but—' He gave a resigned shrug. 'I do it anyway.' To Ferne he added, 'My wife is blind, and she gets very cross if she thinks I'm fussing over her, but I can't help it.'

'Go on home,' Hope told him. 'Just be sure you're at the party tomorrow.'

He embraced her fondly and departed. Almost at once another car appeared and disgorged two young women. One was dark, and so gracefully beautiful that even her pregnancy-bump couldn't detract from her elegance. The other was fair, pretty in a way that was sensible rather than exotic, and was accompanied by an eager toddler.

'This is my wife, Olympia,' Primo said, drawing the pregnant woman forward to meet Ferne.

'And this is my wife, Polly,' Ruggiero said, indicating the fair young woman.

At this distance she could see that Polly too was pregnant, possibly about five months. Her husband's attitude to her seemed protective, and again Ferne was pervaded by the feeling of contentment that she'd had earlier. Just being here, among people so happy to be together, was enough to create it.

It was soon time for lunch. Hope led the way indoors to inspect the meal Elena was preparing, taste things and give her opinion. In this she was joined not only by her daughters-in-law but her sons, who savoured the dishes and offered advice freely—sometimes too freely, as their mother informed them.

'So it's true what they say about Italian men,' Ferne observed, amused.

'What do they say about us?' Dante murmured in her ear. 'I'm longing to know.'

'Why, that you're all fantastic cooks, of course. What did you think I meant?'

He gave a disillusioned sigh. 'Nothing, nothing. Yes, we're all interested in cooking. Not like Englishmen, who eat sausage and mash on every occasion.' Suddenly he looked closely at her face. 'What is it?' he asked. 'Why are you looking troubled?'

'I just suddenly thought—perhaps I should telephone the consulate. They might have some news by now.'

'This afternoon I'll drive you into Naples and we'll visit the consulate here. They can get onto the Milan consulate. Now, let's forget boring reality and concentrate on the important things— enjoying ourselves.'

'Yes, let's,' she said happily.

Dante was as good as his word, borrowing Toni's car after lunch and driving her down the hill through the streets of the old town until they reached their destination near the coast.

There the news was bleak. Neither her passport nor her credit cards had been recovered.

'Considering how quickly they were reported, it looks as though someone made off with them,' Dante observed. 'But hopefully they won't be any use to them.'

'We can arrange a temporary passport,' the young woman at the desk said. 'But it will take a few days. There's a kiosk over there for the photograph.'

'No need, I'll take it,' Dante said. Eyeing Ferne's bag, he added, 'If you'll lend me your camera.'

She handed it to him. 'What made you so sure I had it?'

'You told me you always had it. And the woman who was smart enough to record her lover's infidelity wouldn't miss a trick like this.'

She showed him how to work it, and they spent a few minutes out in the sun while she turned this way and that at his command.

'Pull your blouse down this side,' he said. 'You've got pretty shoulders; let's see them. Good. Now, shake your head so that your hair fluffs up.'

'This is no good for passport pictures,' she objected.

He grinned. 'Who said anything about passport pictures? Maybe I have a wicked purpose of my own.'

Back inside, they switched the camera to 'view' and showed the results to the woman at the desk, who regarded them with saintly patience.

'None of these are suitable. I think you should use the kiosk,' she suggested.

'We could have done that to start with,' Ferne pointed out.

'But then my wicked purpose wouldn't have been fulfilled,' Dante said unanswerably. 'Come on; go into that kiosk and take some shots that make you look dreary and virtuous.'

'Are you suggesting that I'm *not* dreary and virtuous?'

'Which part of that question do you want me to answer?'

'Let's just get on with it,' she said hastily.

When the formalities were complete, Dante took her to a café by the beach and they relaxed over coffee.

'If you think the villa's a madhouse now,' he said, 'wait until tomorrow when the rest of the family get here.'

'There's quite a lot of them, isn't there? Six, I think Hope said.'

'That's right, although they don't all live around here. Luke and Minnie will be coming from Rome. Justin and Evie from England, with Mark, Justin's son, and their baby twins.'

A terrible thought struck Ferne. 'Where will they be staying?'

'At the villa, of course.'

'And you're there too, so whose room have I been given? Someone will end up sleeping on the sofa because of me, and I can't have that. I've got to go.'

'And stay where—in a hotel? With no money or paperwork?'

'Well, if you could lend me some money I'll pay it back…'

Dante shook his head firmly. 'Sorry, no. To tell the hotel that you're a trustworthy person, when actually I don't know if you are, would be most improper. And we must always behave with propriety, mustn't we?'

Despite her agitation, she couldn't help laughing.

'You,' she said in a slow, deliberate voice, 'wouldn't recognise *propriety* if it came up and whacked you on the nose—which I am strongly tempted to do right now.'

'Curses!' he said theatrically. 'She's seen through me. All right, I'll admit my true motive. I plan to keep you here, a prisoner, subject to my will. Cash would help you to escape, which doesn't suit my evil purpose.'

'I wonder if I can guess your evil purpose,' she said dryly.

'Well, I'm not exactly subtle, am I? But do I need to be? You're in my power.'

'In your dreams!' she chuckled.

'In those too,' he said with a yearning look.

'No, I didn't mean— Oh, you know what I meant.'

'Well, a man can dream, can't he?' he asked, eyeing her significantly.

'He can dream all he likes, as long as he doesn't

confuse dreams with reality,' she said, also significantly. 'And you didn't answer my question. Whose room have I been given?'

He didn't reply, but his mouth twisted.

'Oh no, please, don't tell me…?'

'If you feel that way, we could always share it,' he suggested.

'Will you just stop, please?'

'All right, all right, don't eat me. You can't blame a man for trying.'

'I can. I do.'

'You wouldn't if you could sit where I'm sitting, looking at you.'

She gave up. How could you talk sense to a man who had that wicked glint in his eyes?

But it could be fun finding out.

CHAPTER THREE

'IF YOU'RE going to reject me, I'll just have to console myself with those pictures of you that I took,' Dante remarked.

'I deleted them,' she said at once.

'Like hell you did! If you didn't delete the evidence of your lover misbehaving, you aren't going to wipe out the pics of you looking like every man's dream of sexy.'

'Will you stop talking to me like that?'

'Why should I?'

What could she say? *Because it gives me a fizz of excitement that I'm not ready for yet.*

He was a clever man, she reckoned; he made it clear beyond doubt that he was sexually attracted to her, yet with such a light touch that she could relax in his company, free from pressure. She didn't doubt that he would jump into her bed in an instant, if she gave him the barest hint. But without that hint he would sit here talking nonsense, biding his time.

She wondered how many other women had been beguiled into his arms, and what had happened to them when it was over. She suspected that Dante would always be the one to say goodbye, treating love easily, never lingering too long. But there was more to him than that; instinct, too deep to be analysed, told her so.

His tone changed, becoming what he would have called 'prosaic'.

'While I think of it—' he reached into his wallet and handed her a wad of notes '—you can't walk around without any money.'

'But you just said you wouldn't—'

'We're back in the real world. You must have something. Here.'

Staggered, she looked at the amount. 'So much? No, Dante, please—I can't take this.' Accepting some of the notes, she tried to thrust the rest back at him.

'You don't know what you may need,' he said firmly, pushing her hand away. 'But what you will definitely need is your independence, and with that you'll have it. Put it away safely.' He sounded like a school master.

'But what about keeping me in your power?' she asked, tucking it into her bag. 'Making me independent isn't going to help your evil purpose.'

'True,' he mused. 'On the other hand, nothing

gained by force is really satisfying. It's better when she knocks on his door and says she can't live any longer without his wild embraces. Much more fun.'

'And do you think I'm going to do that?'

He seemed to consider this. 'No, I think you'll go to the stake before you yield an inch. But, as I said before, a man can dream.'

They regarded each other in perfect, humorous understanding.

Afterwards they drove back to the villa slowly, where supper was just being prepared.

'Some people only turn up just before a meal,' Francesco jeered, giving Dante a friendly thump on the shoulder.

He'd gone home and returned with his wife, Celia, whom he now drew forward.

Ferne would hardly have guessed that Celia was blind. She was bright and vivacious with a way of turning her head, clearly aware of what was happening around her. They fell easily into conversation, sitting on the terrace and chatting about their work. Celia's career was making the world accessible to the blind.

'I'm working on a scheme to make theatres more friendly,' she said. 'It involves an ear-piece with a description of the action. Francesco and I were in London a couple of months ago, going to lots of shows so that I could get some ideas, and we went to a performance where everyone was going crazy over the star, Sandor Jayley. They said he looked incredibly sexy in a little Roman tunic.

'But Francesco wouldn't tell me that, and I had to find out afterwards when apparently there were some deliciously scandalous pictures of Sandor in the papers. Why, what's the matter?'

Dante had drawn a sharp breath. The sight of his appalled face made Ferne burst out laughing.

'Have I said something wrong?' Celia begged.

'No, not at all,' Ferne choked. 'It's just that…'

Briefly she told the story and Celia covered her mouth in horror.

'Oh no! What have I done? I never meant— Please, please—'

'It's all right,' Ferne hurried to say. 'I saw the funny side of it ages ago. Oh heavens!' She went off into gales of laughter again, then calmed down and tried to reassure Celia that she wasn't in a state of collapse. It took a while, but at last she managed it.

When she looked up Dante was observing her with a strange smile and a look in his eyes that might have been admiration.

From inside the house they heard Hope's voice.

'Ferne, dear, are you there? I need your help.'

'I'll be back in a minute,' Ferne said, hurrying away.

Celia listened as Ferne's footsteps faded, then turned to Dante.

'She's gorgeous,' she said. 'You're a lucky man.'

'What makes you think she's mine?'

'Francesco says you can't take your eyes off her.'

'And with reason. She's worth looking at.'

'I think her face is gentle and kind, like her voice, when she went to so much trouble to reassure me. She sounds lovely.'

'She is lovely,' Dante murmured.

'Is she really all right about that man—the one they call "sexy legs"?'

'Would you mind not saying that?' Dante said in a strained voice.

'You've really got it bad, haven't you?'

'I decline to answer,' he said after a moment. 'Shall we go in to supper?'

That evening was one of the most pleasant Ferne had ever spent. As the sun faded, lights came on in the garden and at last everyone drifted away from the table to drink their wine under the trees.

'I think your family has found the secret of happy marriage,' Ferne murmured. 'They all look like courting couples—even Hope and Toni, after all these years.'

Dante nodded. 'Hope says that's all down to Toni, the sweetest-natured man in the world. He's always been very kind to me. I'm glad he has happiness now, even if it's in the sunset rather than the sunrise.'

'I wonder if that could be better.'

'I doubt it. Who can ever tell what their own sunset is going to be?'

'Perhaps wondering about it is one of the pleasures of life?' she suggested.

He gave a little shrug. 'Perhaps. Let's go where we can watch the Naples sunset.'

Totally content, she let him lead her to a place where they could stand beneath the trees and watch the miracle that was happening over the bay. For a dazzling moment the light was deep red, seeming to set the sea on fire, and they watched it in awed silence.

'No matter how often I see that,' he murmured, 'it never fails. As long as there's so much glory in the world…' He fell silent.

'Have you spent much time here?' Ferne asked.

'Since my parents died I've kind of moved around the family, living with aunts, uncles, grandparents. This was where I came in the summer, and I loved it. It felt more *home* than anywhere else.'

'But it sounds sad to be moving around the family, not really having a settled base.'

'I like having a big family. There's nothing to

compare with the feeling that you have the whole tribe behind you.'

'Isn't there one member of the tribe you need more than the others?'

'Hope and Toni have been like second parents. Apart from them, no. Like you, I'm an only child, but I thrive on having plenty of cousins.'

At last everyone drifted back to the house. There were children to be put to bed, and Hope wanted an early night. Ferne was glad of the chance to go to her room to be alone and think about everything that had happened to her.

To think about Dante Rinucci.

He was attractive, amusing, sexy and clearly in the mood for a diversion. Since she felt the same, there was really no problem, except for the little voice in her head that kept saying, *Beware!*

But beware what? she asked herself.

There's something about him that doesn't add up.

Nonsense. I'm just being fanciful.

She put on a night-gown, took out her laptop and connected it to her digital camera. In a moment she was looking at the pictures Dante had taken of her, trying to recognise herself.

Who was this woman with the come-hither look, giving the man that teasing smile because she was basking in his attention? It was an illusion. Dante had summoned that look from her in the joking spirit that seemed natural to him, and somehow he'd persuaded her to glance sideways, smiling, to intrigue him as he intrigued her. This man was a natural showman with the gift of luring everyone else into the show. There was no more to it than that, and she mustn't forget.

There was a knock on the door and Dante's voice called, 'It's me.'

She drew a slow breath of dismay. She'd half-expected him to appear at her door, but not so soon. Where was the skilled, sensitive man with the light touch that she'd pictured? Was he going to be vulgarly obvious after all? Her disappointment was severe.

As she was preparing the words of rejection, he knocked again. 'Can I come in?'

'Yes,' she said hastily, reaching for her robe and whisking it on as his head appeared cautiously around the door.

'Ah, you've got the pictures on-screen,' he said. 'I was hoping to see them. Am I any good as a photographer?'

'Er, yes, some of the pictures are very nice,' she said, trying to marshal her thoughts.

He was still fully dressed and didn't seem to notice that she was attired for the night. He studied the computer screen eagerly.

'Nice,' he said. 'You photograph well, and the light was good just then.'

He ran through to the end of the pictures, then back, then forward again, until he found one that seemed to please him especially. She had just shaken her hair so that it fell in soft curls about her face, framing her laughter.

'I'd like to have a copy of that one,' he said. 'You look just great.'

Here it was: the first move. *Be careful.*

But it was hard to be careful when she was suddenly conscious of her nakedness beneath the flimsy night-gown. Her whole body seemed alive to him and oblivious to her efforts at control.

'I'm afraid that may take a while,' she said. 'I don't have a printer with me.'

'No problem. Here's my email address. Send it to me as a file attachment and I'll take care of the printing. Now, I should get to bed if I were you. You've had a long day, and tomorrow is going to be even busier.'

He turned in the open door.

'Sleep well. Sorry I disturbed you. Goodnight.'

The door closed behind him.

Just down the corridor, the sound of that door closing was heard by two who lay contentedly in each other's arms.

'Leaving so soon?' Toni observed. 'Dante's losing his touch. Usually he can have any woman he wants—for a little while.'

'I know,' Hope sighed. 'As soon as it looks like getting serious, he vanishes. But how can we blame him? Think what it must be like for him, living with the knowledge that— Oh, it's terrible! Of course he can't be like other people.'

'He won't let anyone mention the subject,' Toni said sombrely. 'If you try, he becomes cold and angry. He wants to pretend that nothing is wrong, but if you catch him off-guard it's there in his eyes, the knowledge and the fear.'

'Should we tell Ferne?' Hope said. 'Just in case?'

'Warn her, you mean? Not now. Perhaps later. Dante would be furious to know that his secret was out.'

'Won't it have to come out in the end?'

'I don't know,' Toni said sadly. 'Perhaps it will never be spoken of at all—until it's too late.'

Dawn was the best part of the day, when the bright, clear air gave the view across the bay to Vesuvius a new vividness. How peaceful the volcano looked now it was sleeping, and how hard won that peace must be. The previous night had taught Ferne that.

She'd thought herself so well prepared, so

ready to fend off any advance from Dante. But when he'd bid her a gentlemanly goodnight she'd been ill prepared for any of the reactions that had coursed through her.

Starting with disbelief, they had exploded through to outrage, deprivation and finally insult. At the mere prospect of making love with him, her body had flowered. And he hadn't been interested. It was sheer bad manners.

She could cheerfully have hurled something at the door he'd closed behind him. It had taken the rest of the night to calm the volcano inside her, and now the sight of the real one in the distance didn't improve her temper.

Had he suspected her moment of weakness? The thought made her go hot and cold.

She felt an urgent need to get away from where he might be. He'd come out last night to watch the sunset. Suppose he came out again at dawn?

Turning to hurry inside, she saw him standing behind her. How long had he been there?

'Good morning,' she said hurriedly, trying to get past him.

But he detained her with a light hand on her arm. 'Stay.'

'You're very free with your commands,' she said tersely.

'Have I offended you?'

'Of course not. But I expect you want to be alone.'

'Not alone from you.'

He turned her so that she faced the sea and then he stood behind her, his arms crossed over her breast, holding her gently against him. Mysteriously his touch seemed to soothe her annoyance, and Ferne put up her hands, not to push him away but to hold his forearms.

'So near and yet so far,' he murmured.

'How far is Vesuvius really?'

'Only about six miles in earthly distance, but it comes from another universe. Once, years ago, I heard it rumble, and it was like magic. I'm always hoping for another one.'

'No luck?'

'Not yet. It keeps you waiting.'

'Maybe it can't decide what it wants.'

'Or maybe it knows what it wants and can't decide what to do about it,' he mused. 'Even when you want something badly, the way isn't always clear.'

Now she had her answer about the night before. He didn't want to keep his distance from her, but for some reason seemed to feel that he should. So the next step was up to her. Nothing else mattered now; she was content.

They returned to find the villa already awakening. Everyone was agog at the arrival of the two remaining sons, Justin from England, Luke from Rome. As many of the family as possible were going to the airport to meet Justin, his wife and children. Dante and Ferne remained at the villa to greet Luke.

In the early afternoon Primo and Olympia arrived, soon followed by another car, out of which stepped a powerful-looking man and a petite, fair-haired young woman.

'Luke and Minnie,' Dante said.

It was clear from the interested looks Ferne was getting that her story had spread throughout the family. When Minnie came downstairs from settling into her room, she commandeered Ferne's company, demanding to be told everything. But before there was time to say much there was a shout and everyone hurried outside to welcome the party from England.

Justin, Hope's eldest son, was an austere-looking man who at first seemed out of place in this convivial gathering, but Ferne noticed that his eyes followed his mother with a possessive look that contrasted curiously with his bearing. He had the same look for his wife, Evie, a brisk young woman with an air of friendly efficiency.

They were accompanied by Mark, Justin's son by his first marriage. He was twenty, handsome, with dark wavy hair and brilliant eyes that made both the young maids give him yearning looks.

'He's just discovering his powers as a ladykiller,' Justin said with a groan, yet also a touch of fatherly pride. 'It makes him very difficult to live with.'

'Don't be hard on him,' Evie protested. 'It's not his fault he's good-looking. He's just finished his first love affair with a girl who teaches ballroom dancing. He started learning as a way of getting close to her, and now he's really good.'

The young man's presence changed the atmosphere, making it livelier. Later, when the meal was over, Toni rummaged through some old tapes, made in the days before rock 'n' roll, and played them on an ancient tape recorder.

'Go on,' he told Mark. 'Let's see how good you are.'

Without hesitating, Mark extended a hand to Ferne, whom he'd been admiring across the table all through supper.

'Dance with me?'

Pleased, she accepted. She was a good dancer, and Mark was an expert. Soon they were spinning around in perfect time.

'Let's go really fast,' he said suddenly, swinging her around and around.

Gasping, she just managed to keep up. When they finished there was applause from the others, who had retired to sit down and watch them with admiration.

'What is that dance?' Dante asked, coming forward hastily. 'Could you teach it to me?'

'It's basically the quick-step,' Mark told him. 'You do it like this.'

Someone switched the music on again, and there were more cheers and applause as Mark gave a dazzling demonstration, with Ferne as his partner. Then Dante took possession of her and proceeded to show how well he'd learned.

Ferne had to admit that he was a natural, mastering the fastest steps with ease, and taking her flying across the floor as if they had been doing this all their lives.

With this partner the most intricate steps became easy to her, and her feet flashed in and out, sometimes between his own feet, so that she felt they must surely trip each other, yet never did. She had the glorious sensation that no mistake was possible while Dante held her. He was a powerful man, but that power lay not in muscles and brawn but in quicksilver.

That was how he lived his life, she was sure. If trouble loomed, he would dance around it, or over it, or past it, then vanish into the shadows, leaving everyone wondering if he'd ever really been there. It made him both enchanting and dangerous.

At last Toni changed the tape, and they slowed into a waltz.

'I'm impressed,' she gasped. 'Have you really never done the quick-step before?'

'No, but I love dancing; the faster, the better.'

'Waltzing's too dull for you, huh?'

'Much. Who needs it? You have to hold her close.'

'As you're doing with me?'

'Naturally. And you have to pay her compliments, like she's the loveliest woman in the room.'

'But you're not doing that!' she protested indignantly.

'Why should I bore you with what you've heard a hundred times before? Besides,' he added more slowly, 'you know exactly what you look like.'

He was right. She'd taken time over her appearance, and was pleased with the result. The honey-red of her hair was perfectly set off by the floaty chiffon dress with its mixture of autumnal colours. It was knee-length, revealing that her legs were long and elegant, her ankles perfect, and she had a natural balance for the high-heeled sandals that many women couldn't have risked wearing.

In the arms of this tall man, those heels were an advantage, helping her match his height and see his face more closely.

'Maybe I know and maybe I don't,' she teased. 'That's for me to say.'

'So you want me to tell you that you're a dream of beauty, a goddess of the night?'

'Oh, shut up!' she chuckled.

'I'm just trying to do the proper thing here.'

'And you're always so proper, aren't you?'

'Well, somebody did once say that I wouldn't recognise propriety if it came up and whacked me. I can't recall her name just now.'

'Ah! One of those instantly forgettable females. She was probably just trying to provoke you to get your attention.'

He gave a self-mocking smile. 'I wish I could believe she wanted my attention.'

'Or she might be playing cat-and-mouse with you.'

'I'd like to believe that too. You don't know what fun cat-and-mouse can be.'

'You think I don't?' she asked, eyebrows arched sardonically.

'No, forget I said that. Of course you do.' He added hopefully, 'You could probably teach me a thing or two.'

'No, I don't think I could teach you anything about playing games.'

'The game of love has many different aspects,' he suggested.

'But we're not talking about love,' she whispered. 'This is a different game altogether.'

It was a game that made her pulses race and her whole body sing from the close contact with his. Reason argued that her physical excitement was due to the movement of the dance, but reason fell silent before the pleasure of his clasp about her waist and the awareness of his mouth near hers.

'What do you call the game?' he whispered.

'I'm sure we each have our own name for it.'

'Tell me yours.'

She glanced up, murmuring, 'I'll tell you mine if you'll tell me yours.'

'I asked first.'

This time she didn't reply, but her look was full of mischief.

'You're going to tease me, aren't you?' he said. 'You're a wicked woman.'

'I know. I work at it.'

'No need. I reckon a certain kind of wickedness comes naturally to you.'

'True. It's one of the great pleasures of life.' Exhilarated, she provoked him further. 'Almost as much fun as cat-and-mouse.'

A gleam of appreciation came into his eyes. 'Cat-and-mouse; I wish I knew which one I was.'

'I'll leave you to work that one out.'

He gave a shout of laughter that made everyone

stare at them, and began whirling her fast again until they spun out onto the terrace, where she broke from him and darted away, running down the steps and under the trees. She was high on excitement, and the sound of him pursuing her was a delight. She ran faster, challenging him to follow her, and he accepted the challenge.

'Woman, are you crazy?' he demanded, winding his arms around her waist in a grip of velvet and steel. 'Just how much do you think a man can take?'

She responded not with words but with laughter, that rang up to the moon until he silenced her mouth with his own. Somehow the laughter continued, because it was there in the kiss, passing from her to him and back again. It was there too in the skilful movements of his hands that knew how to coax without demanding, persuade without insisting.

He had the gift which so many men lacked, of kissing gently. Her return kiss was joyful, curious, teasing just a little.

'I'm not crazy,' she whispered. 'And perhaps a man should exercise a little self-control.'

'Not while you're making it hard for him,' he growled, moving down her neck.

She was unable to say more, because his lips had found the spot where she was most sensitive.

Shivers went through her, defying her efforts to control them as his mouth caressed the hollow at the base of her throat, touching it softly again and again while she clung to him and her head whirled.

He was wicked. Even with all her nerves shouting warnings, he could still make her want him. Her hands had a will of their own. They clasped his head, drawing him closer against her so that his lips continued their skilled work. She should push him away, but, just another minute…

She felt the ground beneath her. She didn't know when he'd drawn her down, but suddenly she was lying in his arms, and he was looking at her with an expression on his face that she couldn't see through the darkness.

That was so like him, she thought feverishly—always keeping one part of himself a secret. And right now she wanted to know his secrets, wanted to know everything about him, to feel his hands on her body, all over, wanted everything there was to want.

His fingers were at the neck of her dress, trying to draw it lower. When it would go no further, he drew the shoulder down and laid his lips against it. Now she could feel his hair brushing her face and she ran her hand deliciously through it, sighing with satisfaction.

But then she heard something that froze her blood: laughter, soft and merry, coming from a little distance away. The family was appearing in the garden, getting nearer.

CHAPTER FOUR

'DANTE,' she hissed. '*Dante*! Get up.'

Frantically she pushed at him and he drew back, frowning.

'They're coming,' she said. 'They mustn't find us like this.'

Muttering a curse, he wrenched himself away and got to his feet, drawing her up with him. He would have run, but Mark's voice came through the trees.

'Ferne, Dante, are you there?'

'I'm going to murder that boy,' Dante muttered. 'He's doing this on purpose.'

'Don't be paranoid.'

'I'm not paranoid,' Dante said in a soft, enraged voice. 'He fancies you.'

Despite her jangling nerves, she nearly laughed.

'Nonsense. His heart's given to his dancing-girl friend.'

'He's twenty,' Dante snapped. 'He forgot her the minute he left England.'

'You don't know that.'

'Of course I know. I've been twenty.'

'So *that's* what young men of twenty do. And thirty. And thirty-five.'

Dante flung her the look of a man driven to madness.

Now the others were calling them. There was no choice but to walk back into the light, looking as cheerful and natural as possible. Ferne had a worrying feeling that her voice was shaking and she was sure that her smile looked unnatural.

But, more than that, she was shaking inside. She felt like someone who'd found herself unexpectedly on the edge of a cliff, and had backed off without knowing how she'd got there.

The family settled down for final drinks under the stars. Mark tried to get close to Ferne but was deterred by a scowl from Dante. If Ferne's nerves hadn't been jangling, she might have felt flattered and amused.

Hope ordered a pot of tea and Ferne drank it thankfully, feeling the warm liquid soothe her. Hope was looking at her kindly, and her eyebrows raised in surprise when Ferne took four sugar-lumps instead of her usual one. She needed them.

'I'm feeling a little tired,' she said as soon as

she decently could. 'You won't mind if I go to bed?'

'I'm tired too, after the flight,' Evie said, and the party began to break up.

Ferne escaped upstairs, unable to meet Dante's eyes. Once in her room, she plunged into an icy-cold shower. That would soon put her right.

It did, to the extent that it cooled down her flesh, but her mind remained as disturbed as before. She was accustomed to thinking of herself as calm and collected. Even in the throes of passion for Sandor she'd felt in command— something which their grande finale had surely proved.

But Dante had upset that unruffled composure, making her wonder if it was really such a virtue. Had she perhaps become a trifle smug? If so, he was rescuing her from that danger, surprising her again and again.

He insisted on haunting her mind, despite her stern orders for him to depart. But that was Dante: awkward. When she stepped out of the shower and caught a glimpse of herself in the mirror, he seemed to be there, eyeing her nakedness longingly, making her regret that she hadn't allowed him to see her, because he would have liked her so much.

She pulled on her nightdress and in her mind's eye his face fell.

'Get out!' she told him. 'Go away and leave me alone.'

He obeyed, but not without a final glance over his shoulder.

There was a soft knock at her door.

'Who is it?'

'It's me,' said Dante.

She nearly said, 'Are you back already?' but stopped herself in time.

'What do you want?'

'Can I come in? There's something I need to talk about.'

She stood back to let him in, first making sure that her robe was securely fastened. Even so, she felt as though her garments were transparent.

He was still in shirt and trousers, but now the shirt had been torn open at the throat, showing several inches of his chest. It was an attractive chest, she had to admit that, but now she was trying to be cautious. In his arms tonight she'd almost lost her head. There had been a moment in the grass when she would have done anything he wanted, because he could make her want it too.

She was sure he knew it. This was one clever, manipulative man, and she must never let herself forget that.

'What did you want to talk about?' she asked demurely.

'Us,' he said at once. 'And what you're doing to me. I don't think I can stand it much longer.'

Now she was glad she'd taken the cold shower, for her body had regained its equilibrium and her mind was able to view him rationally.

'If you can't stand being with me, it was hardly wise of you to come here,' she pointed out.

'I didn't say that,' he replied, imitating her tone of reasoned argument. 'It's the "so near and yet so far" aspect that's shredding my nerves. It should be one or the other, and I thought we might discuss it sensibly and come to a rational decision.'

The bland innocence of his face might have fooled anyone less alive to his tricks than Ferne. But by now she was back in command.

'I quite agree,' she said seriously. 'One or the other. And, since I'll be gone fairly soon, I think it we should opt for the second choice.'

'Pardon?'

'It would be wise for you to leave my room.'

He nodded. 'It would be wise, wouldn't it? If I were a wise man I'd flee and never look back. But I was never wise.'

'Then this would be a good time to start.'

He slid an arm around her waist.

'I know I shouldn't have come,' he murmured. 'But I had to. You were so wonderful tonight. I watched you and knew I had to dance with you—

and then I danced with you and knew I had to hold you in my arms and kiss you and love you…'

He drew her close as he spoke in a grip that was gentle and implacable together.

'That's going a little too far, surely?' she asked lightly.

'But I want to go too far with you. How could I want anything else when you're so beautiful and you fire me up? I want to go too far and then further—'

'Hush,' she said suddenly. 'I thought I heard a noise in the corridor. Could anyone have seen you?'

'Not a soul. Don't worry, I'll be as quiet as a mouse.'

'You, a mouse?' she jeered softly. 'Who do you think you're fooling? Dante, I like you a lot, I really do, but I am not some daft little bimbo to be overcome by your charm. Don't forget, I've been seduced by an expert.'

'Are you suggesting I'm not an expert?' he asked in outrage.

'Well, you're not doing brilliantly right now.'

He gave a sigh and a rueful look, much like a schoolboy caught playing truant. She almost capitulated there and then, but thankfully managed to hold firm.

'It was worth a try, wasn't it?' she teased.

'I don't know what you mean.'

'Like hell you don't! You came in here saying to yourself, "Go on, give it a whirl. She might say yes, she might say no, she might slap my face. Let's find out".'

His sheepish expression confirmed her suspicions.

'Well, I found out, didn't I?' he said. 'But at least I didn't get my face slapped.'

'That's the next stage. Now, depart while we're still friends.'

'Friends? Is that really all you—?'

'*Go!*'

He went. Hastily.

As an attractive woman working in the entertainment business, Ferne had had a fair amount of experience in saying no to over-enthusiastic gentlemen, and she'd discovered that you could tell a lot about a man by how he behaved at the next meeting, assuming there was one. Some behaved well, some badly, some pretended that nothing had happened.

Dante, of course, had to be original, hopping behind her from tree to tree as she walked through the garden, darting out of sight when she turned until she cried, exasperated, 'Come out, you idiot.'

'If you're calling me an idiot, does that mean

I'm forgiven?' he asked, presenting himself hopefully before her.

'I guess it does.'

From behind him came a shout. 'Dante, are you coming?'

'On my way,' he yelled back. 'I'm going into town with Carlo and Ruggiero, but I couldn't go until I knew I was back in favour.'

'I didn't say you were back in favour,' she told him sternly. 'I said you were forgiven—just.'

'Yes, of course, there's a difference. I'll work on it when I get back. Bye.'

He kissed her cheek and fled, leaving her laughing and wondering what she had to do to get the last word.

But then, she reflected, did she really want the last word? It had a melancholy sound.

She spent an enjoyable day with Hope and the other women, talking about England and fussing over the children. Dante's behaviour to her that evening was restrained and impeccable. He seemed completely oblivious to her as a woman, which was how she preferred it, she tried to tell herself.

Ferne had said she was never without her camera, and it was true, so when she came across Toni playing with Ruggiero's baby son she hurried into action and produced some swift, spontaneous shots that had everyone exclaiming with delight.

'I've been thinking what I can do to thank you for your kindness,' Ferne said to Hope. 'And now I know. I'm going to take pictures, dozens of them—everybody alone, in couples, with their children, without their children. Then I want you all to gather in the garden so that I can take a big one.'

'And I'll always have a memento,' Hope cried, overjoyed. 'Oh, yes please.'

Ferne started at once, going around the house, working on her idea until everyone had a solo shot, down to the tiniest child.

To these she added pictures taken secretly, when people had been unaware of being photographed and were therefore more natural. The final result was a triumphant collection that made Hope weep with joy, and give a special dinner in Ferne's honour.

'That was a very kind thing you did,' Dante said as they sipped wine together. 'Hope's family is everything to her.'

His praise made her slightly embarrassed.

'I did it for myself, really. Taking pictures is a kind of compulsion, and when I can't do it I get restless.'

'Why do you put yourself down? Who are you hiding from?'

'Since when were you an expert in psychoanalysis?' she asked, amused. 'I'm not hiding.'

'Some people would say you were hiding behind the camera, getting everyone else into focus but staying safely concealed. I'm just playing with ideas. If you want some good pictures, let me take you into town and show you old Naples, where the historic buildings still exist. You'll find all the pictures you want.'

She agreed eagerly and they went the next day, driving down into the *centro storico*, as historic Naples was called. As he'd guessed, she was enthusiastic and began clicking, enchanted by the narrow, winding streets with washing strung from side to side, and the stalls selling fish and fruit.

At last they collapsed into chairs at a roadside café, and revived themselves on cake and coffee.

'I'm so glad you thought of this,' she sighed blissfully. 'It's been wonderful. This place is almost too picturesque to be true.'

Dante nodded. 'Naples has its modern districts, places full of soulless, efficient buildings. But it also has these corners where people can still be human instead of cogs in a wheel. People here don't just know each other, they're neighbours, practically family. A lot of them *are* family. You tend to get whole apartment-blocks populated by relatives. Let's have some—'

He stopped as a wild scream came from somewhere nearby. Suddenly there was chaos. People were running down the little streets, waving their arms and indicating something behind them.

'*Incendio!*' they screamed. '*Incendio!*'

'There's a fire somewhere,' Dante said.

Following the pointing hands, they began to run until they came to a five-storey building on one side of a narrow alley, where the ground was entirely made of steps. Smoke was billowing from the windows and people were streaming out, shouting to each other.

'They've called the fire brigade,' Dante said, picking up a few words. 'But these lanes are too narrow for the machines. The nearest they'll get is that corner, then they'll have to carry the ladders into this street and set them on the ground. Let's hope their ladders are long enough. Luckily, everyone seems to be escaping the buildings fast.'

Behind them a woman was screaming, 'Piero, Marco, Ginetta, Enrico—*mio dio!*'

From the bags cast aside on the pavement, it seemed that she had been shopping when the news had reached her and had run back to her children. Now they were hurling themselves into her arms and she was sending up frantic prayers of relief.

'*Salvo,*' she wept. Safe. '*Oh, dio! Salvo. Ma no! Dove Nico?*'

Nico? People began to look around. Nico? Where was Nico?

One of the boys said something and recoiled as his mother slapped his cheek.

'What is it?' Ferne asked, horrified.

'Nico was coming down with them, but they lost sight of him,' Dante explained. 'She's blaming them for going on without him.'

'Nico!' the woman screamed, gazing up at the building. '*Nico!*'

Suddenly there was a mighty rumble followed by a crash from inside the building, and smoke billowed out of the windows.

'The inside has collapsed,' Dante said grimly. 'Let's hope Nico got out.'

But the next moment there was a shout of horror. Everyone looked up to see a little boy standing on a rickety wrought-iron balcony at the top, looking down.

'Nico!' his mother screamed again. 'Come down.'

She was too hysterical to realise that this was impossible, but everyone else understood, and groans went up at what seemed inevitable.

People were running to fetch ladders which they leaned up against the wall, but the boy was five storeys up and nothing reached him. Another ominous rumble from within the building warned how close danger was.

'Move that ladder!' Dante yelled. 'Push it over here.'

'But it's not long enough,' someone protested.

'Don't argue,' he roared. 'Just do as I say.'

Impatiently he yanked the ladder from their hands and set it up against the wall.

'Hold it,' he snapped.

Recognising the voice of authority, they scurried to obey. This was a new Dante, one Ferne had never seen before, a man of grim determination; his eyes were hard, his attitude set, brooking no argument, and woe betide anyone who got in his way.

She ventured to say, 'But what will you do when the ladder runs out?'

For a moment he looked at her as though he'd never seen her before.

Then recognition kicked in, and he said curtly, 'I'll climb.'

He turned away without waiting for her reply and the next moment was climbing the ladder swiftly, two rungs at a time, until he reached the base of the third balcony. Seizing the wrought iron, he managed to haul himself to the upper rim while the crowd below gasped. Ferne gazed in awe, thinking how strong his arms must be to manage that.

Having mounted the balcony, he climbed up onto the rail and leapt upwards. It was only a small distance, but it was enough to take him to the base of the next balcony where he did the same thing, managing to climb up there too.

One more to go. Thank goodness, Ferne thought, that he was so tall and so long in the leg. A shorter man could never have managed those leaps.

Now he was there, soothing the child. But how was he going to descend with him? Those watching below saw Dante take a hard, considering look down, then nod as though the decision was made. He turned and knelt down so that the child could climb onto his back; his arms wound tightly about Dante's neck. The next moment he'd swung over the balcony, going down the iron railings inch by inch until he reached the bottom and hung there.

Everyone below held their breath, wondering what he could possibly do now. He soon showed them, swinging back and forth until he could risk releasing the rail, and taking a flying leap onto the balcony below. It seemed an impossible trick, yet he managed it, throwing himself forward at the last minute so that he landed on his knees, and that the child on his back was safe and unhurt.

Nearly done. One more leap before they

reached the safety of the ladder. Could he make it, or would they both plunge to earth? Down below hands were raised up as if everyone feared the worst and would try to catch them.

Dante didn't hesitate, swinging over the balcony, working his way down the railings, then taking the leap. A roar broke from the crowd as he landed safely.

A man had climbed the ladder and now reached out to take Nico, helping him down to safety while Dante remained on the balcony, breathing hard. Cheers and applause broke out as the child reached the ground, but nobody could relax until his rescuer was also safe. At last Dante reached for the ladder and climbed down to a deafening roar.

Ferne felt the tears pouring down her cheeks. She couldn't have said why she was weeping, whether it was fear for Dante or pride in him, but she was filled with feelings that threatened to explode.

He gave her a brief smile and went to the mother, who was in transports of delight, uttering passionate thanks that seemed to embarrass him. She was clinging to the child, who seemed dazed and unresponsive, but who suddenly seemed to awaken and look around him, searching for something. When he didn't find it, he began to scream.

'Pini?' he cried. 'Pini! He'll die—*he'll die!*'

'Is that another child?' Ferne asked. 'Does he mean someone's still in there?'

'No, Pini is his puppy,' said his mother. 'He must be out here somewhere.'

'No, *no*!' Nico sobbed. 'He's still in there. He'll die.'

His mother tried desperately to soothe him.

'*Caro*, it can't be helped. Nobody can risk their life for a dog.'

Nico began to scream. 'Pini! Pini, Pini…!'

'He's probably dead already,' somebody said. 'He must have been overcome by the smoke—he won't have suffered.'

'No, *there*!' came a shout from the crowd.

Everyone looked up, gasping at the sight of the little dog appearing at the window. He was barking and looking around him in fear and bewilderment. Screams rose from the crowd as his inevitable fate approached, and Nico began to struggle, trying to escape.

'Pini, Pini—I'm coming!'

'No!' cried his mother, clutching him tightly.

'Stay there,' Dante said sharply. 'Just don't move.'

The next moment he was running headlong back to the building.

There were more screams from the crowd as they realised what he meant to do.

'He's crazy—does he want to be killed? Does he know what he's doing? Stop him!'

But Ferne had seen the reckless determination in his eyes and knew that nothing could have stopped him. Terrified, she watched as he reached the house and began climbing up the ladder through the smoke that now seemed to surround everything. Every time he vanished, she was convinced she wouldn't see him again, but somehow he always managed to reappear, higher and higher, closer to the place where the dog was looking down, yelping with terror.

By now two fire-engines had arrived, but had to stop at the end of the narrow street. Seeing what was happening, the firemen came running along the street with a detachable ladder and sent it shooting up towards Dante. Mercifully it was longer than the first one, but when they shouted at him to climb onto it he merely glanced down at them, shook his head and turned back, heading up again.

He'd reached the last balcony, but now his luck ran out. As soon as he seized it, the wrought iron pulled away from the crumbling brickwork so that one end came completely free, swinging down violently. Screams came from the crowd as Dante hung from the iron, seemingly with no way to save himself. The firemen were working the ladder, trying to get it closer to him.

Ferne watched, her heart in her mouth, unable to endure looking, yet equally unable to turn away. It was surely impossible that he could come through this alive?

Then he kicked against the wall hard enough to swing out and up. From somewhere he found the strength to reach higher, and begin to climb up the swinging balcony. He did it again and again, inching closer to the window where the dog was shivering.

Cheers rose as he finally made it, but as he reached for the dog the animal vanished into the building. Dante hauled himself in, also vanishing, and everyone below held their breath. The next moment there came a crash from inside. Smoke billowed from the window, and an appalled hush fell over the onlookers. He was dead. He must be.

Ferne buried her face in her hands, praying frantically. He couldn't die. He mustn't.

Then a shout of triumph went up. *'There he is!'*

Dante had reappeared at another window, further down, with the dog in his arms. Now he was closer to the ladder with the fireman at the top. A little more manoeuvring, and it was near enough for him to reach down and hand the animal to the fireman, who began to back down the rungs, leaving the top of the ladder free for Dante to follow.

It was nearly over. He reached the ladder,

climbed onto it and started the descent. In another moment, he would be safe.

But then something seemed to halt him. He froze and stayed there, clinging on, leaning against the metal, his eyes closed, his head hanging down.

'Oh heavens, he's passed out!' Ferne whispered. 'It's the smoke.'

The fireman passed the dog to another man further down, then climbed back up to Dante, positioning himself ready to catch him if he fell, reaching up to touch him.

To everyone's relief Dante seemed to come out of his trance and look around him. At last he managed to move and complete the journey down.

As he reached the ground, the cheers broke out again. He shook his head as though to clear it and, seeming to return to reality, took the dog from the fireman and carried it to the child, who screamed in ecstasy.

If the crowd had cheered him before, they now went completely mad. A man who risked himself for a child was a hero; a man who took the same risks for a dog was a wonderful madman.

Yes, a madman, Ferne thought, trying to still her thumping heart. A glorious madman, but still a man who didn't live on the same planet as everyone else.

He seemed strangely unwilling to enjoy the praise he'd won. They tried to hoist him shoulder-high, but now all he wanted was to escape.

'Let's go,' he said, grasping her hand.

CHAPTER FIVE

THEY ran from the crowd, dodging the outstretched hands, darting through street after street until they were lost and their pursuers were far behind.

'Where are we?' she asked.

'Who cares? Anywhere.'

'And where's the car?'

'Anywhere. What does it matter?'

'Will you talk sense?' she laughed. She was on a high of relief.

'No. Why talk sense? When was it ever sensible to be sensible?'

'Never for you; I can see that,' she said tenderly. 'Come on, let's get you somewhere safe.'

'Wherever you say. Lead on.'

She suddenly felt protective. Taking his hand as she might have taken the hand of a child, she led him until they found a small café with a table on the pavement where they could let the sun drench them.

'I need this,' he said, 'after all that smoke. I also need a drink, but I suppose I'd better not have one since I have to drive home—when we find the car.' He began to laugh. 'Where are we going to find it? Where do we start?'

'I think I remember the street. Don't worry about it now.'

When the waiter had taken their order, he leaned back, looking at her. There was exhilaration in his eyes.

'Dante, for pity's sake,' she said, taking hold of his hand again. 'Will you come down to earth?'

'I thought that was what I'd just done.'

'You know what I mean. You're up in the stratosphere somewhere. Come back down to the same planet as the rest of us.'

'What for? I like it up here.' He turned his hand so that now he was holding her. 'Come up here with me. It's a great life. I've never had such fun.'

'Fun? You could have died!'

'Well, the strangest things can be fun if you look at them the right way.'

'You could have died,' she repeated slowly, as if to an idiot.

'But I didn't. I could have, but I didn't. Don't you understand? It's been a great day.'

'How can you *say* that?' she exploded. 'How can you sit there as if it was nothing? Of all the mad things to do! To save a child, yes, that's wonderful. But to take such a risk for a dog—what were you thinking of?'

'I'm a dog lover. And that little boy would have been broken-hearted if I'd left his dog to die.'

'And what about you? Don't you mind if you live or die?'

He shrugged. 'I don't worry about it. It'll happen when it happens.'

'It'll happen a lot sooner if you take crazy risks.'

'Maybe it will, maybe it won't. What's wrong with taking risks? Life's better that way. Think of it as doing the quick-step with fate as your partner. You go faster and faster, never knowing which of you is going to reach the edge first. Everything is possible; it's the only way to live. And, if not, better to die like that than, well, some of the other ways.'

'You nearly came to grief,' she reminded him. 'When you were on top of the ladder you seemed to collapse. You just clung there and I thought you were going to fall. What happened?'

'Nothing. You imagined it.'

'But I didn't. You slumped against the ladder.'

'I don't remember. There was smoke everywhere and a lot of things passed me by. It doesn't matter now. Let's leave it.'

'I don't think we ought to leave it. You may have been affected in some way that isn't obvious yet. I want a doctor to have a look at you.'

'There's no need,' he said in a voice suddenly full of tension. 'It's over.'

'But you don't know that,' she pleaded. 'You passed out on the top of that ladder and—'

'How the hell do you know?'

The sudden cold fury in his voice was like a slap in the face, making her flinch back.

'You weren't up there; you don't know what happened,' he snapped. 'You saw me close my eyes against the smoke and give myself a moment's rest before climbing down the rest of the way. *And that's all!* Don't start dramatising.'

'I didn't mean— I'm just worried about you.'

'Do I look as if I need worrying about?' he asked in a voice that was now quiet and steely.

Ferne was struggling to come to terms with the terrible transformation in him, and she had to take a deep breath before she could reply bravely, 'Yes, actually, you do. Everyone needs worrying about. Why should you be any different? Something dreadful has happened to you. It might have made you ill and I simply want to find out. Why should that make you angry?'

'Why does any man get angry at being fussed over? Just leave it, please.'

His voice was still quiet, but now there was something in it that was almost a threat.

'But—'

'I said *leave it*.'

She didn't dare to say any more, and that word 'dare' told her what a dreadful thing had happened. The mere thought of being afraid of Dante was incredible, and yet she was. This was more than masculine irritation at being 'fussed over', it was bitter, terrifying rage.

But he was recovering himself. Before her eyes, the temper drained out of him.

'I'm sorry,' he said. 'I'm not quite myself. I'll be all right soon. Just promise me one thing—you won't say anything about this at home.'

'Not tell them about the fire? I think that story will get around somehow.'

'I don't mean that. I meant the other thing, that I had a bad moment on the ladder. Hope worries easily. Say nothing.'

When she hesitated he said, 'You *must* give me your word.'

'All right,' she said quickly. She had a fearful feeling that his rage was on the verge of rising again.

'You promise faithfully?'

'Yes, I promise.'

'Fine. Then everything's all right.'

Everything was far from all right, but she couldn't say so. She could never forget what she'd seen.

But now his mood was lightening, changing him back into the Dante she knew.

'Look on the bright side,' he said. 'Think what exciting pictures I must have given you.'

Pictures. Stunned, she realised that she'd never once thought of them.

She, to whom photography was such a part of her DNA that even her own lover's treachery had been recorded for posterity, had forgotten everything the moment Dante had started to climb.

'I didn't take any pictures,' she whispered.

'What do you mean?' he asked in mock outrage. 'You take pictures of everything. How come I'm not considered worth the trouble?'

'You know the answer perfectly well,' she snapped. 'I was too worried about you to think of photography.'

He shook his head. 'I don't know what the world is coming to,' he said sorrowfully. 'My great moment and you missed it. Shall I go back up and give you a second chance?'

'Don't bother,' she said crisply. 'The second take is never as effective as the first.'

They both knew what they were really talking about. The woman who let nothing get in the way of a good picture had missed this because she'd forgotten everything but his being in danger.

Now he would know, and how he would love that! But when she met his eyes she saw in them not triumph, but only bleak weariness, as though a light had gone out. He was struggling to present his normal, jokey self, but it was an effort.

'Come on,' he said tiredly. 'Let's go home.'

They found the car and drove back in silence. At the villa he immediately went for a shower. While he was away, Ferne outlined the events to the family but, remembering her promise, said nothing about what had happened at the end.

'Trust Dante to go back for the dog,' Hope said.

'He loved it,' Ferne said. 'It was as though risking his life gave him some sort of kick.'

'His father was the same,' Toni sighed. 'Always finding excuses to do crazy things.'

'Yes, but—' Hope began to speak, then stopped.

Puzzled, Ferne waited for her to continue. Then Hope met her husband's eyes and he gave an almost imperceptible shake of the head.

'If a man is like that, he's like that,' she finished lamely. 'I'll just go up and see if he's all right.'

She returned a moment later saying, 'I looked in. He's asleep. I expect he needs it.'

Then she deftly turned the conversation, leaving Ferne again with the impression that where Dante was concerned there were strange undercurrents.

Next morning he'd already left for town when she rose. She tried not to believe that he was avoiding her, but it was hard.

Her new credit cards arrived in the post, and news came from the consulate that her passport was ready. She drove down and collected it, then went to a café by the water and sat, considering.

Surely it was time to move on? Her flirtation with Dante had been pleasant but it would lead nowhere. Forgetting to take pictures was an ominous sign, because it had never happened before. But the mere thought of a serious affair with him was madness, if only because of his habit of withdrawing behind a mask.

On the surface he was a handsome clown who could tease his way into any woman's heart. But, when she'd given him her heart, what then? Would she be confronted by the other man who concealed himself inside, and whose qualities were beginning to seem ominous? Would he frighten her? Or would Dante keep her at bay, allowing her only to see what suited him? Either prospect was dismaying.

She thought of their first meeting on the train when they had sat together, thundering through the night, talking about the circles of heaven and hell. It had seemed a trivial conversation, but now she had the conviction that Dante was mysteriously acquainted with hell. Yesterday he had looked into its fiery depths not once but twice. Unafraid. Even willing.

Why? What did he know that was hidden from the rest of the world? What was his hell, and how did he confront it?

She was sunk so deep in her reverie that it took a while to realise that her mobile phone was shrieking.

'Ferne—at last!'

It was Mick Gregson, her agent, a cheerful, booming man.

'You've got to get back here,' Mick said. 'There's a great job coming up, big time, and I've put your name forward.'

He outlined the job which was, indeed, 'big time'. Following Sandor's example, a major Hollywood actor had just signed up for a West End play, seeking the prestige of live theatre. Next to him Sandor Jayley was peanuts.

'The management wants only the best for the pics, and when I mentioned you they were very interested.'

'I'm surprised anyone wants me after last time,' she observed wryly.

'I've heard that they value your "self-sacrificing honesty". Don't laugh; it's doing you a world of good. Seize this chance, sweetie. Gotta go.'

He hung up.

So there it was, she thought, staring at the silent phone: the decision was made for her. She would say farewell to Dante and return to England, glad to have escaped.

Escaped what?

She would have to learn to stop wondering about that.

The phone rang again. It was him.

'Where are you?' he asked in a voice that sounded agitated. When she told him, he said, 'Don't move. I'll be there in a few minutes.'

She was waiting for him, baffled, when he drew up at the kerb.

'Sorry to hassle you,' he said as she got in. 'But I need your help urgently. I've had a call from a man who owns a villa a few miles away and wants me to sell it. I'm going up there now, and I need a great photographer, so of course I thought of you.'

'I'm flattered, but my experience is showbiz, not real estate.'

'Selling a house can be a kind of showbiz, especially a house like this. In the nineteenth century, it was notorious. The owner had a wife and three mistresses and kept each one in a different wing. Then he was murdered.'

'Good for them.'

He laughed. 'It's odd how people always assume that it was the women.'

'If it wasn't, it should have been,' Ferne said without hesitation.

'It probably was. The police never found out. I want you to bring out the drama, while also making it look a comfortable place to live.'

After an hour they came to the villa, set on a hill with an extravagant outline, as though it had been built as part of a grand opera. Inside, the place was shabby with few modern comforts. The owner, a tubby, middle-aged man, followed her around, pointing out what he considered the attractions, but she soon left him behind and made her own way. The atmosphere was beginning to get to her.

It took three hours. On the way home, they stopped off for a meal and compared notes. Now Dante was a serious businessman. His notes were thorough, and he was going to do a first-class job with the house.

'My text, your pictures,' he said. 'We're a great team. Let's get back home and put it all on my website.'

'Fine, but then I've got something to tell—'

'Naturally, I'll pay you.'

'So I should hope.'

'Of course, I can't afford your usual fees. I expect you get top-dollar now for the *right* kind of picture.'

'I'll ignore that remark.'

'But you're the best at this kind of thing, and I could sell these houses much faster with your help.'

'I'm trying to tell you—'

'I'm going to leave soon, driving all over this area, drumming up business. Come with me. Together we'll knock 'em all dead.' When she hesitated, he took her hands in his. 'Say yes. It's time to have a little fun in your life.'

This was the Dante she'd first known, the chancer who faced life with a smile. The darkness of the recent past might never have been.

'I don't know,' she said slowly.

She was more tempted than she wanted to admit. Just a little longer in his company…

'Look, I know what you're thinking,' he said persuasively. 'But you're wrong. I've accepted your rejection.' His voice became melodramatic. 'Bitter and painful though it is.'

Her lips twitched. 'Oh, really?' she said cynically.

'Why don't you believe me?'

The mere idea of Dante meekly accepting rejection was absurd. It was a ploy, telling her that he was settling in for a long game, but if she admitted that she would be conceding a point in that very game. If there was one thing she knew she mustn't do, it was let him win too easily.

'Are you seriously asking me to believe that you'll act like a perfect gentleman at all times?'

'Ah, well, I might not have been planning to go quite that far,' he hedged cautiously. 'But nothing to offend you. Just friendly, I promise.'

'Hmm,' she observed.

'Hmm?' he echoed innocently.

'Hmm.'

In this mood, he was irresistible. On the other hand there was the promise of the biggest job of her life, maybe a trip to Hollywood eventually.

'I'll think about it,' she said.

'Don't take too long.'

They drove back to the villa and spent a contented hour at the computer, marrying his text and her pictures. The result was a triumph, with Ferne's flair for the dramatic balancing Dante's factual efficiency. He sent a copy to the owner, who promptly emailed back, expressing his delight.

At the end of the evening Ferne went out onto the terrace and stood looking up at the stars, wondering what she was going to do. It should have been an easy decision. How could any man compete with such a career opportunity?

She knew what would happen now. Dante would have seen her come out here, and he would follow her, trying to charm her into doing exactly what he wanted.

Just *friendly*, indeed! Who did he think he was kidding?

She could hear him coming now. Smiling, she turned.

But it was Hope and Toni.

'Dante has gone to bed,' Hope explained. 'He wouldn't admit it, but I think he has a headache.'

'Is something wrong?' Ferne asked. Something in the older woman's manner alerted her.

'He tells us that he wants you to travel and work with him,' Hope said.

'He has asked me, yes. But I'm not sure if I should agree. Perhaps it's time for me to be getting back to England.'

'Oh no, please stay in Italy for a while,' Hope said anxiously. 'Please go with him.'

Ferne's first thought was that Hope was match-making, but then she got a closer look at the other woman's expression and her amusement died. Hope's face was full of strange fear.

'What's the matter?' she asked. 'It's something serious, isn't it?'

Again that disconcerting silence; Hope glanced at her husband. This time he nodded and she began to speak.

'I'm going to confide in you,' she said, 'because we trust you, and we both think that you must learn the secret.'

'Secret?' Ferne echoed.

'It's a terrible one and it weighs on us. We try not to believe it, but the truth is—' She took a deep breath and spoke with difficulty. 'The truth is that Dante might be dying.'

'What?' Ferne whispered, aghast. 'Did you say—?'

'Dying. If that should happen, and we could have done something to prevent it and had not— But he will not have it spoken of, you see, and we don't know what to do.'

Ferne forcibly pulled herself together.

'I don't understand,' she said. 'He must know if he's ill or not.'

She could hear fearful echoes in her head. They were filled with warnings and told her that she was about to discover the dark secret that made Dante unlike other men.

'On his mother's side, he's a Linelli,' Hope explained. 'And that family has a hereditary problem. There can be a weak blood vessel in the brain that can suddenly start to bleed. Then the victim will collapse, perhaps go into a coma, perhaps die.'

'This has happened to several of them over the years,' Toni said. 'Some have died, but even the ones who survived have often been unlucky. His Uncle Leo suffered a major haemorrhage. His life was saved by surgery, but his brain was damaged. Now he's little more than a child, and to Dante he's an awful warning. He refuses even to consider that he might have inherited this illness and need treatment.'

'But has there ever been any sign?' Ferne asked. 'Or are you just afraid because it's hereditary? After all, not everyone in the family will have it.'

'True, but there was one frightening moment about two years ago. He had a headache so bad that he became confused and dizzy. This can mean a minor rupture of the blood vessel, and if that's ignored it can lead to a major one. But he insisted that he was perfectly recovered, and nothing else has happened since. That might mean nothing is wrong, or it might mean that he's been very, very lucky. He could go on being lucky for years, or…' Hope broke off with a sigh.

'But wouldn't it be better to find out?' Ferne asked.

'He doesn't want to know,' Toni said sombrely. 'He isn't afraid of death, but he is afraid of surgery, in case he ends up like Leo. His attitude is that, if death comes, it comes.'

'Doing the quick-step with fate,' Ferne murmured.

'What was that?'

'Something I've heard him say. I didn't understand it before. But I can't believe he'll go so far. Surely he'll be better having a diagnosis?'

'He's determined not to,' Hope said in despair. 'He doesn't want the family pressuring him to have surgery, even though it might not be so much of a risk. Surgical techniques have greatly improved since Leo's operation nearly thirty years ago, and Dante could easily come out of it well and whole, but he won't take the chance. He wants to get the best out of life while he can, and then, well…'

She gave a despairing sigh. Ferne was transfixed. This was worse than anything she'd feared.

'If only we knew for sure, but there's no way to be quite certain,' Hope resumed. 'Unless there's a definite symptom, like a dizzy spell. Have you ever seen him grow faint without warning?'

'Yes,' Ferne said, remembering with horror. 'He seemed to get dizzy when he was coming down the ladder when he saved the dog. But it seemed natural after what he'd been through—all that smoke.'

'It probably was natural,' Hope agreed. 'And his headache tonight is probably natural, just a delayed reaction to what he went through. But we always wonder. It's hard to say anything for fear of enraging him.'

'Yes, I've seen that,' Ferne murmured. 'I wanted him to see a doctor, and he was very angry. He made me promise not to say anything to the family, or I would have told you before. He got so furious that I had to give in. I could hardly believe that it was him.'

'He's going off alone,' Hope said. 'Please, Ferne, go with him.'

'But what could I do? I'm not a nurse.'

'No, but you'd be there, watching out for him. If anything worrying happens, you won't dismiss it as a stranger would. You can summon help, perhaps save his life. And you might even persuade him that he doesn't have to live this way.'

'He won't listen to me,' Ferne said. 'He'll probably suspect me from the start.'

'No, because he's invited you to go with him, so it will all seem natural to him. Please. I beg you.'

Ferne knew the decision had been made. This woman who had come to her rescue and asked so little in return was now imploring her.

'You don't need to beg me,' she said at last. 'Of course I'll do it. You must tell me all you can about this illness, so that I can be of most use.'

For answer, Hope flung her arms about Ferne's neck in a passion of thankfulness. Toni was more restrained, but he laid a powerful hand on Ferne's shoulder and squeezed tightly.

But Ferne was shaking, wondering what she'd let herself in for.

CHAPTER SIX

A SOUND from inside the house made them look up quickly, but it was only Primo, come to say goodnight before taking Olympia back to their apartment. Ferne took the chance to slip away among the trees. She needed to calm her thoughts and, more than that, calm her emotions.

For now there was a howling wilderness inside her, and she wanted to scream up to the heavens that it couldn't be true. It mustn't be true, for if it was true she couldn't bear it.

She'd wanted to know Dante's secret, and here it was. He was probably dying, and he knew it. At any moment of the day or night he could collapse without warning. That was the fact he lived with, refused to duck from, even laughed at. That was the quick-step he was dancing with fate.

Now she understood why he'd gone back into the burning house when anyone wiser would have stayed away. Inwardly he'd been yelling, 'Go on, then, do your worst!' to the gremlins who haunted him, trying to scare him, not succeeding.

If he'd died that day, he'd have called it a blessing compared with the fate he dreaded: permanent disability, being as dependent as a child, pity. To avoid that he would do anything, even walk into the fire.

This was why he chose light relationships. He couldn't allow himself to fall in love, nor would he risk a woman falling in love with him. He was at ease with her because she fended him off with laughter and seemed in no danger of serious feelings, which was just what he liked; it was safer for them both.

But he'd miscalculated, she thought in anguish. The news of his being in danger had brought a rush of emotion to her heart. Deny it though she might, the misery of knowing that he might be brutally snatched from her at any moment was tearing her apart.

She should fly this place now, run from him while she might still have even a little control over her feelings. Instead she had agreed to stay in his company, to watch over him, vulnerable to his charm which seemed even more potent now that she understood the tragedy that lay behind it.

She would probably fall in love with him despite her determination not to. And how would she bear what might happen next?

Flee! said the voice in her mind. *Forget what you've promised.*

'I can't,' she whispered, resting her head against a tree.

To go was to abandon him to whatever was waiting, leave him to face it alone. The fact that he'd chosen it that way would make it no less a betrayal.

'No,' she murmured. 'No, no, *no!*'

Suddenly she knew she couldn't keep her promise to Hope. She'd been mad to say yes, and there was still time to put it right. She would hurry back now…

'There you are,' came Dante's voice. 'Why are you hiding?'

She turned to see him walking towards her. He had the rumpled look of a man who'd recently been asleep.

'I came out for some air,' she said. 'It's lovely out here at night.'

'It is beautiful, isn't it?'

He didn't put his arms about her, but leaned against the tree, regarding her quizzically.

'Are you all right?'

'Yes, fine,' she said hastily. 'What about you? How's your head?'

'There's nothing wrong with my head. Why do you ask?'

'When you went to bed early, Hope thought—'

'Hope's a fusspot. My head is fine.'

Was his voice just a little bit too firm? She shouldn't have raised the subject. It was a careless mistake, and she must be more careful.

'You can't blame her for fussing,' she said lightly. 'You of all men, going to bed early! What kind of earthquake produced that?'

'I'm probably still suffering a touch of smoke inhalation. Even *I'm* not superman.'

'Now, there's an admission!' she said in as close to a teasing voice as she could manage.

She longed to take his face between her hands, kiss him tenderly and beg him to look after himself. But anything like that was forbidden. If she stayed she would have to guard every word, watch and protect him in secret, always deceive him. The sooner she was out of here, the better.

'Dante,' she said helplessly. 'There's something I must—'

'Oh yes, you were trying to tell me something this afternoon, weren't you? And I never gave you the chance. Too full of myself as always. Tell me now.'

It would have to be faced soon, but before she could speak blessed rescue came in the form of a commotion. Ruggiero's toddler son, Matti, came flying through the trees as fast as his short legs would carry him. From behind came Ruggiero's voice, calling to him to come back, which he ignored.

'I used to escape at bedtime just like that,' Dante said, grinning. 'Some rotten, spoilsport grown-up always grabbed me.'

He seized Matti and hoisted the toddler up in his arms, laughing into his face.

'Gotcha! No, don't kick me. I know how you feel, but it's bedtime.'

'It was bedtime hours ago,' Ruggiero said breathlessly, reaching them. 'Polly looked in on him and he made a run for it.'

'Parents can be a pain in the neck,' Dante confided to the tot. 'But sometimes you have to humour them.'

Reluctantly Matti nodded. Dante grinned and handed the child to his father.

'You really know how to talk to him,' Ruggiero said. Then, fearing to be thought sentimental, he added, 'I guess it's because you're just a great kid yourself, eh?'

'Could be,' Dante agreed.

Ferne, watching from the shadows, thought that there was more to it than a joke. Dante was part-child, part-clown, part-schemer, and part something else that she was just beginning to discover. Whatever it might turn out to be, he was a man who needed her protection. Somewhere in the last few moments the decision had been made.

'Now we're alone again,' he said, 'what were you going to say?'

Ferne took a deep breath and faced him with a smile.

'Just that I really enjoyed working with you. When do we leave?'

Be careful what you say in jest: it may return to haunt you.

That thought pursued Ferne over the next few days.

She'd teased Dante about being a perfect gentleman at all times, and he'd responded with an encouraging dismay. But as time passed she began to realise that he'd taken her seriously and was being, as he'd promised, 'just friendly'.

He bought a car, a solid, roomy vehicle designed for serious travel, and quite unlike the frivolous choice she might once have expected him to make. They headed south to Calabria, the rugged, mountainous territory at the toe of the Italian peninsular. One of Dante's techniques was to seek out places that had been on the market for a long time and offer his services.

'There are three villas there that my research

tells me have been for sale too long,' he said. 'Let's try our luck.'

Their luck was in. The owners were getting desperate and were eager for Dante to add their properties to his books. They spent several days working up a sales pitch for each house, complete with glorious pictures. At the end of it, Ferne was exhausted.

'I seem to spend my life climbing stairs and walking mile-long corridors,' she complained. 'If I'd known it was going to be this tiring, I wouldn't have come.'

Dante himself didn't seem at all tired, and was clearly in such blazingly good health that she wondered if she was crazy to be watching out for him. He had a fund of funny stories which he directed at her over dinner, reducing her to tears of laughter, after which he would take her hand to lead her upstairs to their separate rooms, kiss her on the cheek and bid her goodnight.

No man could have behaved more perfectly. No man could have been more restrained and polite. No man could have been more infuriating.

For this she'd turned down the chance of a lifetime?

Mick Gregson hadn't been pleased.

'What were you thinking of?' he'd bawled down the phone. 'This man carries influence in film land. If he'd liked your work, you could have done anything you wanted.'

But I'm doing what I want, had been her silent thought.

'Ferne, I can't go on representing you if you're going to act like this.'

'That's your decision, Mick, and of course I respect it.'

They had parted bad friends.

Now she was on the road with a man who'd promised 'just friendly', and who seemed infuriatingly determined to keep his word.

There was no justice.

But one thing had changed—now she understood the true reason for Dante's restraint. He wouldn't make advances to her because his personal code of honour forbade him to ask for love when he might die without warning.

Here was the explanation for the way he slipped quickly in and out of relationships, never getting too close to any woman. It was his way of being considerate.

And he was right, she assured herself. If she wanted more from him, that was her problem.

'Where do we go next?' she asked as they turned north again, leaving Calabria behind.

'A place near Rome that I've promised to take a look at. There are some two-thousand-year-old ruins, plus a huge villa that the owner insists on calling a *palazzo*, that's "only" six centuries old. It may not be easy to shift.'

'If it's antique and historical, won't the atmosphere of romance help to sell it?'

'An atmosphere of romance is all very well in theory, but people tend to want decent plumbing as well. I know the owner, Gino Tirelli, and he assures me that it's in a good state of repair—but he might, just possibly, be biased. Luckily I'm not due there until next week, so we can give ourselves a few days by the sea.'

'That sounds lovely. This heat is really getting to me.'

'Of course, we could always go sight-seeing in Rome. There are some really interesting historical buildings.'

'The sea, the sea,' she begged faintly.

He laughed. 'The sea it is, then. Let's go.'

A few hours' driving brought them to the Lido di Ostia, the beach resort about fifteen miles from Rome. It was a sunny place of level, pale-yellow sands that were adorned not only with umbrellas and loungers but the other trappings of civilization: wine bars and cafés.

Their hotel was close to the sea with a view over the ocean.

'They've got single and double rooms available,' Dante told her after a talk at the desk. 'A double room's cheaper.' In reply to her raised eyebrows, he said, 'How long can a man behave perfectly?'

'I think I can afford a single room.'

'You don't give an inch, do you?'

'You'd better believe it,' she said, laughing.

Not for the world would she have admitted her relief that his defences were finally crumbling.

The hotel had a shop that sold beach items. She lingered over a bikini that—for a bikini—was relatively modest, and a respectable one-piece. Dante eyed her hopefully as she hovered between them.

'Why don't you try it?' he suggested, indicating the one-piece.

She was slightly surprised that he urged her to try the modest garment rather than the revealing one. Afterwards, she realised that she should have been more suspicious.

In the dressing-room she donned the costume, regarded herself in the mirror and sighed. It was elegant and showed off her figure, but didn't do her total justice. No one-piece could have done that. But, until she was sure how far along this road she was going to let Dante whirl her, she couldn't risk being a tease. That wouldn't be fair to him.

Nor was it fair on her, she realised, trying to calm the pleasure that fizzed through her as she thought of his eyes dwelling on her nearly naked body. It wasn't the only pleasure she was denying herself right now, and soon she must decide why.

She dressed again and went out, handing the costume to the assistant for wrapping. 'I'll take this.'

'I've already paid for it,' Dante said, whisking it out of her hand and putting it into a bag he was carrying. 'Now, let's be off.'

'I can't let you pay for my clothes,' she said as they crossed the road to the beach. 'It wouldn't be proper.'

'If we're going to have another discussion about propriety, I'd rather do it later over champagne.'

'Oh, all right.'

The sand was glorious, soft and welcoming. He hired a hut, two loungers and a huge umbrella, then handed her the bag with her purchase and stood back to let her enter the hut first.

When she opened the bag, she was reminded that this man was a talented schemer.

'They've given me the wrong costume,' she said, going outside again. 'Look.' She held up the bikini. 'But I don't see how it happened. I saw you put the other one into the bag.'

'I guess this one must have already been in there,' he said, eyes wide and innocent.

'But how…?' Light dawned and she stared at him indignantly. *'You didn't?'*

'If you've learned anything about me, you know that I did,' he said unanswerably. 'I bought the bikini while you were in the changing room.'

'But how dare you?'

'A case of necessity. You were going to buy that middle-aged thing that doesn't do you justice, so I paid for them both and slipped the bikini into the bag before you came out.'

'But what about the one I chose? Where is it?'

'No idea. It must have escaped.'

'You—you devious—'

'No such thing. Just a man who doesn't like wasting time. Now, are you going to get in there and change, or are you going to stand here all day talking about it?'

'I'm going to get in there and change,' she said promptly. And vanished.

It might not have been modern and liberated to let a man make her decisions, but that was a small sacrifice in return for the look in his eyes. He'd behaved disgracefully, of course, but all things considered she would forgive him.

The mirror in the hut promised everything to the beauty who gazed back, wearing just enough to be decent. Restrained as the bikini was, it didn't hide the way her tiny waist developed into curved hips, or the fact that her skin was perfect. Turning, she studied her rear view over her shoulder, noting that perhaps her behind was a fraction too generous.

Or, then again, perhaps not.

At last she was ready to make her grand entrance. Throwing open the door, she stepped out into the sunlight, only just resisting the temptation to say, 'Ta-Da!'

He was nowhere to be seen.

Oh, great!

'Ah, there you are,' he said, appearing with cans of liquid. 'I've been stocking up on something to drink. We can keep these in the hut until we're ready.'

'Do I look all right?' she asked edgily.

'Very nice,' he said in a courteous voice that made her want to thump him.

But his smile as he studied her told another story, so she forgave him.

While she waited for him to emerge, she let her eyes drift over the other men on the beach. Sandor had once told her that there were few men who appeared at an advantage in bathing trunks. He'd spoken with self-conscious grandeur, from the lofty heights of physical perfection.

But when Dante appeared she forgot everything else. He didn't show off; he didn't need to. His tall, lean figure was muscular without being obvious, and he seemed to have the tensile strength of whipcord.

Ferne's brief contacts with his body had hinted at power, not flaunted but always in reserve. Now she saw the reality and it pleased her, especially the long legs that moved with a masculine grace that hinted at his ability as a dancer.

For a moment she was back in his arms as they danced across the floor, feet between feet, spinning and twirling with never an inch out of place, because his control had been perfect. Watching him now, his body almost naked, she felt again the excitement of that night begin in the pit of her stomach and stream out to her finger-tips.

'Shall we go in?' he asked, reaching out.

She took his hand and together they ran down the beach, splashing into the surf. She yelled aloud with ecstasy as the water laved her, and joined him in a race out to the horizon.

'Careful,' he said. 'Don't go too deep.'

But she was beyond caring. The feel of the water was so good that she wanted more and more.

'*Yee-haa!*' she cried up to the sky.

He laughed and plunged after her, keeping

close, ready for the moment when she pulled up, treading water and puffing.

'All right now?' he called. 'Got it out of your system?'

'No way. Here goes!'

Kicking hard, she projected herself up as high as she could go, then dropped down deep into the water, down, down, until at last she kicked to start rising again.

But she was deeper than she'd guessed, and she didn't seem to be climbing fast enough. She became alarmed as her breath began to run out.

Suddenly there was an arm around her waist and she was being yanked up to the surface fast, until mercifully her head broke free and she could breathe again.

'All right, you're safe,' came Dante's voice. 'What were you thinking of, you crazy woman?'

'I don't know—I just wanted to— Oh, goodness!'

'Steady. Relax. I've got you.'

He trod water while keeping her well above the surface, holding her tight against him, his hands almost meeting about her waist.

'All right?' he said, looking up.

'Yes, I—I'm fine.'

It was hard to sound composed when the sensation of her bare skin against his was so disturbing. Her thighs were against his chest, his mouth was just below her breasts, and the waves were moving them about so that their contact constantly shifted; with every new touch the tremors went through her.

'I'm going to let you down,' he said. 'You can't touch the ground, but don't worry. Just hold onto me. Down—easy.'

She knew he meant only to be gentle and reassuring by lowering her slowly, but the feeling of her flesh gliding against his was just what she didn't need right now, she thought frantically. Control. *Control*.

'Ouch!' he said.

'What?'

'You're hurting me, digging your nails into my shoulders.'

'Sorry!' she said wildly. 'Sorry—sorry.'

'OK, I believe you. Let's get back to shore. Can you swim, or will you hold onto me?'

'I can manage fine,' she lied.

They made it back to the shore without incident, and she set her feet down on the sand with relief.

'All right?' Dante asked.

'Yes, thank you. You can let me go now.'

'I'll just support you until we reach the lounger. You had quite a shock.'

Her legs felt weak, but that was natural after her

alarm. It surely couldn't have anything to do with her burning consciousness of his left hand about her waist while his right hand clasped hers?

What happened next was really annoying. By sheer ill-luck an unevenness in the sand made her stumble so that Dante had to tighten his grip to stop her falling.

'Let's do it the easy way,' he said, lifting her high into his arms and carrying her the rest of the distance.

This was even worse. Now she had no choice but to put her arms about his neck, which positioned her mouth close to his and her breasts against his chest, something a sensible woman would have avoided at all costs.

At last he eased her down onto the lounger and dropped on one knee beside her.

'You gave me a fright,' he said. 'Vanishing below the water for so long. I thought you'd gone for good.'

'Nonsense,' she said, trying to laugh it off. 'I'd have been bound to float up eventually.'

'Yes, but it might have been too late.'

'Then it's lucky for me that you were there. You do the "rescuing damsels in distress" thing really well.'

'It's my speciality,' he said lightly. 'And, just to show you how good at it I am, let me dry you off.'

He tossed the towel around her shoulders and began to dab.

'I can manage, thank you,' she said in a strained voice.

'All right. Do it properly, and I'll get you something to drink.'

He poured her some wine in a plastic container.

'Sorry it's a bit basic, but the wine is good,' he said.

She drank it thankfully, wishing he'd move away and not kneel there, so kind, so sweetly concerned, so nearly naked.

'Thanks,' she said. 'I feel better now. You don't need to hover over me.'

'Am I being too protective? I can't help it. I keep thinking what it would have been like without you, and I don't like that thought at all.'

'Really?' she asked quietly.

'Of course. How could I manage without your brilliant pictures?'

'My pictures?'

'You really enhance my work in a way that nobody else has managed to do. We make a great team, don't you think?'

'Fantastic,' she agreed dismally.

'So I'll just keep on watching out for you.'

Her head shot up. 'What—what did you say?'

'I said I'm watching out for you. You obviously

need someone being protective. Hey, careful. You've spilled wine all down yourself.'

She seized the towel out of his hands and dabbed at her bare torso. Her head was in a whirl, and her senses were in an even worse whirl.

'Did you say you're keeping a protective eye on me?' she said.

'I think I need to, don't you? And it's what friends do, isn't it?'

'Oh yes, of course they do,' she babbled.

'It's time you had a rest.'

'Yes,' she said with relief. 'I think that's what I'll do.'

CHAPTER SEVEN

SHE was glad to escape by stretching out and closing her eyes. His words had unnerved her, reminding her that it was she who was supposed to be watching out for him.

She dozed for a while and awoke to find herself alone. Dante was further down the beach, kicking a rubber ball around with some boys. For a while she watched him through half-closed eyes, unwillingly admiring the lines of his body, the athletically graceful way he moved.

She was no green girl; Sandor hadn't been her first lover. At twenty-eight, she knew her own body well, knew how it could be most totally satisfied, knew exactly what it wanted.

But that could be a problem when it couldn't have what it wanted.

It would have been easier to observe Dante leaping about the beach if she didn't have to listen to the voice inside whispering how well he would move in bed, how subtle and knowing his caresses would be.

How fine would his tall body feel held close against her own long body? When she saw him give a mighty kick, she thought of his legs between hers. When he reached for the ball at an impossible angle, she could almost feel his hands against her skin, exploring her tentatively, waiting for her with endless patience, knowing exactly how to…

She sat up, trembling and annoyed with herself. What was the matter with her?

'Just friendly'. That was the matter.

When Dante returned, he found her fully dressed.

'I've had enough of this,' she said fretfully. 'I think I'll go into town.'

'Great idea,' he said. 'I'll show you the shops, then we'll go to dinner.'

She ground her nails into her palm. Why couldn't he at least show some ill temper, like any other man, thus giving her the chance to feel annoyed with him?

But the wretch wouldn't even oblige her in that.

Because he wasn't like any other man.

At least she'd made him put his clothes on.

They spent the rest of the day sedately, buying the odd garment, and also buying computer software. In one shop she discovered a superb programme that she hadn't expected to be available for another month, and snapped it up. Over dinner, she enthused about it to Dante, who listened with genuine interest. It was the high point of the day.

On reflection, she thought that said it all.

Afterwards he saw her to her door but made no attempt to come in.

'Goodnight,' he said. 'Sleep well.'

She went in, restraining herself with difficulty from slamming the door.

Furiously she thought of the signals he'd sent out that day, signals that had said clearly that he wanted her and was controlling it with difficulty. But the signals had changed. Now he might have been made of ice, and it was obvious why.

He was scheming. He wanted her to be the one to weaken. If either of them was overcome with desire, it must be her. In his dreams, she succumbed to uncontrollable lust, reaching out to entice him.

Hell would freeze over first!

Next day they promised themselves a lazy time in the sun.

'I could happily stay here for ever,' Dante said, stretching out luxuriously. 'Who cares about work?'

It was at that exact moment that a voice nearby called, '*Ciao*, Dante!'

He started up, looked around, then yelled, *'Gino!'*

Ferne saw a man in his fifties, dressed in shirt and shorts, advancing on them with a look of delight on his broad face.

'Is that…?'

'Gino Tirelli,' Dante said, jumping up.

When the two men had clapped each other on the shoulder, Dante introduced Ferne.

'Always I am pleased to meet English people,' Gino declared. 'At this very moment, my house is full of important English people.'

'So that's why you asked me to delay my arrival,' Dante said. 'Who've you got there? Members of the government?'

'A film company,' Gino said in an awed voice. 'They're making a film of *Antony and Cleopatra* and shooting some scenes in the ruins in my grounds. The director is staying with me, and of course the *big* star.'

'And who is the big star?' Ferne asked, suitably wide-eyed.

Before Gino could reply there was a squeal from behind them, and they all turned to see a young man of about thirty with curly, fair hair and a perfectly tanned body strolling along the beach in a careless way, suggesting that he was unaware of the sensation he created.

But he was fully aware of it, as Ferne knew.

Sandor Jayley always knew exactly what effect he was creating.

'Oh no!' she breathed.

'What is it?' Dante asked her in a low voice. 'Good grief, it's—?'

'Tommy Wiggs.'

The young man came closer, pulling off a light shirt and tossing it to a companion, revealing a muscular body sculpted to perfection, now wearing only a minuscule pair of trunks. Regarding him grimly, Dante was forced to concede one thing: as Ferne had said, he did have magnificent thighs.

'I've got to get out of here before he sees me,' she muttered. 'That'll really put the cat among the pigeons.'

But it was too late. Sandor had seen his host and was starting up the beach towards him, doing a well-honed performance of *bonhomie*.

'Gino,' he called. Then, as he saw Ferne, his expression changed, became astonished, then delighted. 'Ferne! My darling girl!'

Arms open wide, he raced across the sand and, before she could get her thoughts together, she found herself enfolded in a passionate embrace.

It was an act, she thought, hearing the cheers around them. For some reason he'd calculated that this would be useful to him so he was taking what he wanted, selfishly indifferent to the effect it might have on her. For she was terrified in case she reacted in the old way, the way she now hated to remember.

Nothing happened. There was no pleasure, no excitement. Nothing. She wanted to shout to the heavens with joy at being free again!

'Tommy—'

'Sandor,' he muttered hastily. Then, aloud, 'Ferne, how wonderful to see you again!' He smiled down into her eyes, the picture of tender devotion. 'It's been too long,' he said. 'I've thought of you so often.'

'I've thought a few things about you too,' she informed him tartly. 'Now, will you let me go?'

'How can you ask me to do that when I've got you in my arms again? And I owe you so much.'

'Yes, those pictures didn't do you any harm, did they? Let me *go*!'

Reluctantly he did so, switching his attention to Gino.

'Gino, how do you come to know this wonderful lady?' he cried.

'I've only just met her,' Gino said. 'I didn't realise that you two were—are…'

'Let's say we're old friends,' Sandor said. '*Close* friends.'

Ferne became awkwardly aware of Dante standing there, arms folded, regarding them sardonically. After everything she'd told him about Sandor, what must he be thinking?

A little crowd was gathering around them as news went along the beach that the famous Sandor Jayley was among them. Young women sighed and regarded Ferne with envy.

'Sandor,' she said, backing away from him, 'Can I introduce you to my friend, Signor Dante Rinucci?'

'Why, sure.' Sandor extended his hand. 'Any friend of Ferne's is a friend of mine.'

Dante gave him an unreadable smile.

'Excellent,' he said. 'Then we're all friends together.'

'Let's all sit down.' Sandor seated himself on her lounger and drew her down beside him.

He was in full flood now, basking in the warm glow of what he took to be admiration, oblivious to the fact that one of his audience was embarrassed and another actively hostile.

'Just think,' he sighed. 'If that house where we were going to shoot had come up to scratch, we'd never have moved to Gino's *palazzo* and we—' he gave Ferne a fond look '—would never have found each other again.'

'There were rats,' Gino confided. 'They had to find somewhere else fast, and someone remembered the Palazzo Tirelli.'

'Why don't you join us?' Sandor said suddenly. 'That's all right with you, isn't it, Gino?' Asking the owner's permission was clearly an afterthought.

Far from being offended, Gino nearly swooned with delight.

'And it will give Ferne and me the chance to rekindle our very happy acquaintance,' Sandor added.

'Sandor, I don't think—' Ferne protested quickly.

'But we have so much to talk about. You don't mind if I take Ferne away from you for a few days, do you?' he asked Dante.

'You mean Dante isn't invited too?' Ferne asked sharply. 'Then I'm not coming.'

'Oh, my dear, I'm sure your friend will understand.'

'*He* may, I won't,' Ferne said firmly. 'Dante and I are together.'

'So loyal,' Sandor cooed in a voice that made Ferne want to kick him in a painful place. 'Signor Rinucci, you're invited too, of course.'

'How kind!' Dante said in a voice that revealed nothing. 'I'll look forward to it.'

Ferne turned horrified eyes on him. 'Dante, you don't mean that?' she muttered.

'Of course I do. Getting really acquainted with the place may help me with the sale.'

'How? You've never needed it before.'

'Well, perhaps I have my own reasons this time,' he said, his eyes glinting.

Sandor didn't hear this exchange. Champagne had arrived and he turned to lift two glasses, one of which he handed to Ferne, saying, 'It's all settled, then. Here's to our reunion!'

A young girl detached herself from the swooning crowd on the beach and asked him for an autograph, handing him her lipstick so that he could write his name on her back. Beaming, he obliged, then gave Ferne a questioning look.

'No camera today? Not like you.'

'I left it in the hotel.'

'You? The lady who never moves without her camera? Well, well.'

His look was heavily significant, clearly meant to recall the last time she had turned her camera on him. She faced him back, her eyes full of anger.

Dante watched them and said nothing.

Having established the scene, Sandor didn't linger over the champagne. Indicating the crowd, he said modestly, 'You see how it is—wherever I go. I'll leave now, and see you at the villa this evening.'

He strode away, pursued by adoring fans, plus Gino.

'So that's him,' Dante said. 'He's exactly as you said, except worse.'

'I don't know what's going on here,' she said

wildly. 'When we last met, he couldn't find words bad enough for me.'

'But that was three months ago, and he did pretty well out of it. He's a bigger star now than he was before, thanks to you. So clearly he wants to shower you with his favours. Tonight you'll be his honoured companion.'

'Are you trying to be funny?' she asked stormily. 'Do you think that's what I *want*?'

He gave a strange smile. 'Let's say I'm interested to find out. I didn't mean to offend you. Let's get going.'

It was late afternoon when they reached the Palazzo Tirelli, a magnificent edifice. Grander still were the ruins that lay nearby, dating back nearly two-thousand years. Ferne could just make out a film crew looking them over, making notes, rehearsing shots.

Gino came to meet them and show them over the place with its long, wide corridors and stone arches. In every room he was able to describe some notable historical episode, which sounded impressive until she saw Dante shaking his head.

Their rooms turned out to be on different corridors, the only ones left, according to Gino. His manner was awkward, and Ferne guessed he was acting on instruction.

At supper she was seated next to Sandor, with

Dante on the opposite side of the table several feet down. There were about fifty people at the long table, most of them film crew and actors. Everyone was dressed up to the nines, making her glad she'd chosen the softly glamorous dress of honey-coloured satin that paid tribute to her curves, yet whose neckline was high enough to be tantalising.

'Beautiful,' Sandor murmured. 'But why aren't you wearing that gold necklace I gave you? It would go perfectly with that dress.'

'I'm afraid I'd forgotten it,' she said.

His self-assured smile made her want to thump him. She glanced down the table to see how Dante was taking it, but he wasn't looking at her.

He was having a good evening. Dinner jacket and bow-tie suited him, as the ladies nearby made clear. Ferne would have signalled her admiration if she'd been able to catch his eye, but he seemed happy with the full-bosomed creature who was laughing so uproariously at his jokes, that her attractions wobbled violently in a way that Ferne thought extremely inappropriate.

For a moment, she was nostalgic for Dante's jokes; sharing laughter with a man brought a special closeness. It was something she'd never known with Sandor, and it meant that she was always on Dante's wavelength, always inhabiting his world, even when they were bickering. In fact, the very bickering was a sign of that closeness, because they could always trust each other to understand.

As Dante had predicted, Sandor treated her as his honoured guest.

'I owe you so much, Ferne. If it hadn't been for what you did for me, I'd never have got the next step up.'

'That's not what you said at the time,' she observed wryly.

'I didn't appreciate your skill in turning a difficult situation into something that would benefit me.'

She stared at him, wondering how she'd ever taken this conceited booby seriously.

'Sandor, what are you after?' she demanded.

He regarded her soulfully. 'Destiny works in mysterious ways. We were fated to meet on that beach. Everyone was staggered by those pictures you took of me. Between us, we produced something of genius, and I think we could be geniuses again.'

She stared at him in outrage. 'You want me to…?'

'Take some more, as only you can. We'll go out to the ruins, and you tell me exactly how you want me to pose. I've been working out in the gym.'

'And I'm sure you're as fit and perfect as ever.'

'What did you think when you saw me today?' he asked eagerly.

It would have been impossible to tell him the truth, which was that he had seemed 'too much', because her ideal was now Dante's lithe frame.

To her relief, the maid appeared to change the plates for the next course. For the rest of the meal she concentrated on the elderly woman on her other side.

Afterwards the great doors were opened onto the garden, where coloured lights hung between the trees. People began to drift out to stroll beneath the moon. Sandor drew Ferne's arm through his.

The crowd congregated near the ruins, where blazing lights had been switched on, illuminating them up to the sky. The director, an amiable man called Rab Beswick, hailed Sandor.

'I like this place more every time I see it,' he said. 'Just think what we can make of these…' He indicated several walls, some of which stood at right angles to each other with connecting balconies.

'Just the right place to make a speech,' came a voice behind them.

It was Dante, appearing from nowhere.

'Antony was known for his ability to make the right speech at the right time,' he said. 'And his genius for picking the place that would be most effective.'

The director looked at him with awe.

'Hey, you're Italian,' he said, as though nothing could be stranger than finding an Italian in Italy. 'Are you an expert about this?'

'I've made a particular study of Marc Antony,' Dante said.

'Well, I'd be glad of anything you could tell me.'

'Let's not get carried away,' Sandor interrupted peevishly. 'This film isn't meant to be an historical treatise.'

'Certainly not,' Dante said suavely. 'Its selling point will be the personal charms of Signor Jayley.'

From somewhere there was a smothered choke. Sandor turned furious eyes in a vain attempt to detect who was making fun of him. Unable to locate a suspect, he turned back to Dante.

Which was what Dante had intended, Ferne thought. Whatever was he up to?

'Height is always effective,' Dante continued smoothly. 'If Antony was to make a great speech up there, silhouetted against the sky—'

'That's not in the script,' Sandor said at once.

'But it could be written in,' Dante pointed out. 'I'm not, of course, suggesting that you yourself should go up there. That would be far too dangerous, and naturally the film company won't want to risk their star. A double could be used for the long shot.'

Sandor relaxed.

'But it could look something like this…' Dante finished.

Before anyone realised what he was doing, he slipped out of sight, and a moment later reappeared on one of the balconies.

'You see?' he called down. 'What a shot this would make!'

'Great!' the director called up.

Ferne had to admit that Dante looked magnificent, standing high up, bathed in glittering spotlight. She only prayed that the balcony was strong enough to hold him and wouldn't start crumbling.

This time she really wished that she'd brought her camera, but one of the production staff had his and was snapping away madly. Sandor was livid, she was fascinated to notice.

'Come on down and we'll talk about it,' Rab called. 'Hey, be careful.' Dante was hopping down like a monkey, ending with a long leap to the floor, where he finished with a flourish.

'You're right, that's a great shot. You'll help us work on it, won't you?'

'Sure thing,' Dante said. 'I can show Mr Jayley how to—'

'It's getting late,' Sandor said hastily. 'We should be going inside.'

'Yes, let's go and look at the pictures,' Rab said eagerly. 'Come on, everyone.'

As the rest of them drifted away, Ferne murmured to Dante, 'What did you do that for?'

'You know exactly what I did it for,' he murmured back. 'I haven't enjoyed myself so much for ages. He's ready to kill me.'

His whole being was flooded with brilliance, as though he'd reached out, taken life by the hand and was loving every moment.

'Didn't anyone ever tell you not to repeat a trick?' she asked severely. 'Just because you climbed up into that building the other week, doesn't mean you have to keep doing it. You were just showing off.'

He grinned, and her heart turned over. 'You won't insult me by calling me a show-off. Too many have said it before you. As for repeating the trick? Sure, it was the memory of the fire that gave me the idea. It was actually a lot easier to get up there than it looks, but your lover wouldn't have tried it if you'd offered him an Oscar.'

'He is not my lover.'

'He wants to be.'

'Come on,' someone yelled from the retreating crowd. 'They're going to show the pictures.'

She would have argued further, but he slipped his arm about her, urging her forward irresistibly until they reached the villa, where someone had linked up the camera to a computer and had projected the pictures onto a screen.

There was Dante, high up, splendid, laughing down at them. Whether his triumph lay in making the climb, or in making Sandor look absurd and diminished, only Ferne knew. One thing she was sure of—he'd done it in style.

She looked around for Sandor, wondering how he was taking this.

'He retired,' Gino explained. 'He's had a long day.'

Translation: he's sulking like a spoilt child, Ferne thought. Dante had hit the bull's eye.

Dante himself seemed oblivious to his success. He was deep in conversation with Rab, and by now Ferne was sufficiently in tune with his mind to recognise that this was another move in the game. He wouldn't say anything in front of an audience. But later…

'I've had a long day too,' she said. 'Goodnight.'

She slipped away and hurried up to her room. Sooner or later there was going to be a visitor, and she wanted to be ready.

First she needed a shower to wash the day off her. She turned it on as hard as she could and stood there, head back, arms wide, just letting it happen. It felt good.

She could have laughed aloud when she thought of how Dante had achieved his revenge—an Italian revenge—not violent, but skilled; a lithe, dancing movement, a quick thrust of the stiletto, unseen by anyone but his adversary, who had slunk away, humiliated.

Now she realised that she ought to have feared for Dante's safety when he'd been up high, but she hadn't, because she was under the spell he cast. And she was still under his spell, she thought happily.

She finished under the shower, pulled a robe around her and stepped out into the bedroom. But what she found there made her stop sharply.

'Sandor!'

He was leaning against the door, his arms folded, a look of happy expectation on his face. He'd removed his shirt so that his magnificent chest was presented for her approval in all its naked perfection, smooth, muscular, evenly tanned.

'What are you doing here?' She sighed.

'Oh, come on, sweetie. We both knew this was going to happen.'

'Tommy, I swear, if you try to touch me I'll thump you so hard you'll see stars.'

'You don't mean that.'

'Don't tell me what I mean. I'm warning you.'

He laughed and sauntered easily over to her, the king claiming his rights.

'I think I might just put that to the test— *Aargh!*'

He yelped as her hand struck his face.

'You bitch!' he wailed. 'I could get a swollen lip.'

She opened her mouth to reply, but before she could speak there was a knock on her door. She darted to open it and found Dante standing there. He was wearing dark-blue pyjamas, and his face had an innocent look that filled her with suspicion almost as great as her relief.

'I'm so sorry to trouble you,' he said, 'but there's no soap in my bathroom and I wondered if you'd mind— Oh dear, am I disturbing something?'

'Nothing at all,' Ferne said. 'Mr Jayley was just going.'

Dante regarded Sandor with apparent surprise, seeming not to have noticed him before, but Ferne wasn't fooled. He knew exactly what he was doing. In his own way, he was as much of an actor as Sandor, but a more subtle one.

'Good evening,' he said politely. 'Oh dear, you seem to have suffered an injury. You're going to have a nasty swollen lip.'

'Eh!' Sandor yelped. He tried to make for the bathroom, but Dante was blocking his way so that he was forced to turn away and retreat from the room altogether, slamming the door behind him.

'That should keep him occupied,' Dante said with satisfaction.

CHAPTER EIGHT

'BUT how did you know? I didn't hit him that hard. He didn't have a swollen lip.'

'No, but he was afraid of it. I was just outside the door and I heard everything.'

'And was it coincidence that you were there?'

'Certainly not. I was lurking in the corridor. When I saw him go in, I listened. After all, you might have welcomed him.'

'And then you'd have just gone away, I suppose?' she said sardonically.

Slowly Dante shook his head, and there was something in his eyes she'd never seen before.

'No way. If you'd welcomed him, I'd have come in and thumped him myself a lot harder than you did. But there was no need. You dealt with him very efficiently——I'm glad to say,' he added softly.

'You didn't really think I wanted him, did you?'

He made a wry face. 'I hoped not, but I

needed to know. When I saw how easily he entered, I did wonder.'

'I was in the bathroom, or he'd never have got in.'

'Are you really over him?'

'Of course I am. I just wish we'd never come here.'

'You were a big hit at dinner.'

'You weren't doing so badly yourself,' she flung at him.

'Just passing the time, keeping an eye on you, making sure you didn't misbehave. I had to know how you feel about him. It mattered.'

'And now you know.' She met his gaze, silently urging him on.

But the man who'd dismissed his enemy with a master stroke suddenly seemed to lose confidence.

'What happens now?' he said. 'It must be your decision. Do you want me to go?'

'I don't know what I want,' she said distractedly. It was almost true.

'Ferne.' His voice was quiet and suddenly serious. 'If you don't know, neither of us knows.'

'That's not fair.'

'Fair?' His voice was edgy. 'You stand there half-naked, doing heaven knows what to me, and *I'm* being unfair?'

The towel robe had opened just enough to show her breasts, firm and glowing with the need she could no longer hide. While she hesitated, he took the edges of the material and drew them apart, revealing the rest of her nakedness.

'*That* is being unfair,' he said in a shaking voice.

She couldn't move. Her whole being seemed to be concentrated on him, on his touch and the thought of where it would alight next. The feeling was so intense that it was as though he was already caressing her everywhere. It was almost a shock when he laid his fingers lightly at the base of her throat, leaving them there, seeming to wait for something.

She drew a long breath. None of Sandor's dramatic caresses had affected her one tenth as much as Dante's patience.

'Tell me,' he said softly.

'Tell you…?'

'Tell me what to do. Ferne, for pity's sake, if you want me to stop say so now, because I don't have that much control left.'

Her smile was deliberately provocative. 'Perhaps a man can have too much control. Maybe he even talks too mu—'

Her words were silenced by his mouth on hers. It was too late now, past the point of no return. Her own kiss was as fervent as his, speaking of desire held in too long, of frustration released in giddy, headlong joy.

While he kissed he was pulling at the robe until it fell to the floor and there was no barrier to his hands caressing her everywhere, setting off tremors that shocked her with their intensity. She managed to return the compliment, ripping away at his clothes until he was as naked as she.

Neither of them knew who made the first move to the bed. It didn't matter. They were running down the same road, seeking the same triumphant destination.

She had anticipated his skill, but her imagination had fallen far short of the reality. He made love as he did the quick-step, unfailingly knowing the right touch, the right movement, always in perfect understanding with his partner. Her body felt as though it had been made for this moment, this loving, this man, and only this man.

At the last moment he hesitated, looking down into her face as though seeking one final reassurance. By now her breathing was coming fast, and any delay was intolerable. She wanted him and she wanted him *now*.

'Dante,' she whispered urgently.

He gave a quick sigh of satisfaction, hearing something in her voice that he'd needed to know, and the next moment he was inside her, glorying in being part of her.

After he looked different. The teasing clown who enchanted her was also the lover who instinctively knew the secrets of her body and used them for his purpose in a way that was almost ruthless. He'd known what he wanted and been determined to have it, but what he'd wanted was her joyful satisfaction. Now he had it, which meant he knew his power over her, but she had no fears about that power. She trusted him too much for that.

She wondered if she looked different to him too. Then she caught the faint bewilderment in his eyes and knew that she did. That delighted her, and it was she who moved towards him for their second loving, caressing him in ways that had never occurred to her before, because he was like no other man. He laughed and settled himself against her, implicitly inviting her to do whatever she liked, an invitation she accepted with vigour.

Later, when they had recovered, he propped himself on his elbow, looking down at her lying beneath him with a mixture of triumph and delight.

'What took us so long?' he whispered.

How could she give him an honest answer when she was only just now facing the truth in her own heart?

It took time because I've been holding back, fearful of having too many feelings for you. I knew if I got too close I was in danger of loving you, and I don't want to. To love you is to risk heartbreak, and I don't have the courage. Even though—even though it may already be too late. Too late for me? Too late for you?

There was no way to say that.

She just opened her arms and drew him in so she could enfold him protectively until they fell asleep in the same moment.

As the first touch of dawn came into the room, Dante rose from the bed, careful not to waken her, and went to stand by the window. From here he could see the sun rising behind the ruins, casting its promise over the new day.

A new day. It was a feeling he'd thought he would never know. The circumstances of his life had bred in him a wary detachment, making it easier to stand back, observe himself wryly, often cynically, and sometimes with a melancholy that he fought with laughter.

But this morning the melancholy had lifted. Detachment was gone, leaving him at peace.

Peace: the very last quality he associated with Ferne. She teased him, haunted him, jeered and provoked him. Sometimes he wondered if she'd known how she tempted him, but then he would see the look in her eye—assessing, challenging, taking him to the next stage of the game they were playing.

The game was called 'who will blink first?' She'd played it with consummate skill, enticing him into indiscretions like buying her a bikini. That had shown his hand too obviously, and she'd played on it, luring him to the edge, closer to the moment when he'd had to abandon the control that ruled his life.

The luck of the devil had been on her side. Nobody could have predicted the arrival of Sandor and the fierce jealousy that had stormed through Dante. Seeing them together on the beach, Sandor's hands actually touching her body—the one he thought of as his own personal possession—he'd come close to committing murder.

She'd tried to refuse the invitation to stay here, but why? A demon had whispered in his ear that she was afraid to be in Sandor's company lest the old attraction overwhelm her. He'd insisted on accepting, driven by the need to see more of them together and know what he was up against.

It had been no satisfaction that so many lures had been cast out to him last night. There were at least three bedrooms at which he could have presented himself, sure of a welcome. Instead he'd haunted her door until inevitably Sandor had appeared, bare-chested, for seduction, and entered without knocking.

The moment when he'd heard her slap the man's face had felt like the beginning of his life.

It meant that in the game they were playing she'd won and he'd lost. Or possibly the other way around. Whatever! He couldn't have been happier.

He returned to the bed, sitting down carefully so as not to disturb her. He wanted to watch her like this, relaxed and content, breathing almost without making a sound. A wisp of hair had fallen over her face and he brushed it back softly. Somehow his hand stayed, stroking her face.

Her lips moved in a smile, telling him that she was awake. The smile turned into a chuckle and she opened her eyes to find him looking directly into them.

'Good morning,' he whispered, settling beside her and drawing her close.

No passion now, just her head on his shoulder in blissful content, body curled against body, and the sense of having come home to each other.

'Good morning,' she murmured.

'Is everything all right?'

'Mmm!' She hid her face against him.

'Me too,' he agreed. 'Very much all right.'

After a while she opened her eyes again to find him sunk in thought.

'What are we going to do now?' he wondered.

'Leave this place behind,' she said at once. 'Sandor will throw us out anyway.'

'A pity. Part of me wants to stay around for a while just to poke him in the eye. He had his turn making me jealous. Now it's my turn to pay him back.'

'Jealous? You?'

'Don't play the innocent. You knew exactly what you were doing to me. You loved seeing me on hot coals.'

'I'll admit it had its entertaining moments,' she mused. 'But that was because you were trying to play hard to get. Not always successfully, mind you, but you tried.'

'Of course,' he said, sounding shocked. 'Don't forget that I promised "just friendly", and a gentleman always keeps his word.'

'Gentleman? Huh!'

'Let's have that discussion later,' he said hastily. 'The point is, I couldn't break my word, so I had to get you to break it for me. You forced me into retreat, so I'm innocent.'

'Oh, *please*!' she jeered. 'The one thing I can't imagine is you being innocent. You are a scheming, manipulative, double-dealing, tricky— Oh, the hell with it! Who cares if you're a bad character? What are you *doing*?'

'What does it feel as if I'm doing? Hush now, while I prove what a bad character I am.'

Laughing, he proceeded to do exactly that with such vigour that she was left breathless.

'I suppose I ought to be grateful to Sandor,' Ferne said when they had recovered. 'He might be a clumsy oaf, but he did us a favour. Do you know, he actually wanted me to take some more pictures of him?'

'What, after you…?'

'Yes, apparently my photographs flattered him as nobody else's did. Heavens, how did I ever fancy myself in love with that twerp?'

He suspected another reason why Sandor had tried to seduce Ferne. Such was the man's vanity that he wanted to believe that he could reclaim her whenever he liked. But about this Dante stayed tactfully silent.

'I suppose we should get up,' he said at last. 'It's a beautiful day.'

Gino was waiting for them downstairs, clearly on hot coals.

'Sandor had a restless night and he's gone for a walk in the grounds. He says he doesn't feel up to seeing anyone.'

'I wonder what could have brought that on?' Dante said sympathetically.

'Artistic sensibility,' Gino sighed.

'I understand,' Dante said solemnly. 'A true artist sometimes needs to be alone to commune with the universe. Did you speak?' This was to Ferne, who was displaying alarming symptoms of choking. She managed to shake her head and he continued. 'We'll leave at once. Give me a call when the filming has finished and I'll come back then.'

They didn't even stay for breakfast. Tossing their things into bags, they fled the Palazzo Tirelli like children making a dash for freedom.

As the car swung out of the gates Ferne caught a glimpse of a tragically noble figure standing on a hill, watching their departure with a look of passionate yearning. Not that she could see his expression at this distance, but she would have bet money on it.

'It's like your Shakespeare said,' Dante observed. 'Some men are born twerps, others achieve twerphood, and some have it thrust upon them. Well, something like that, anyway.'

'You've really got your knife in to Sandor, haven't you?' she chuckled.

Dante grinned. 'I did once. Not any more.'

Ferne leaned back in her seat, smiling. The jokey note of the conversation suited her exactly. This was a man to have fun with, nothing more. The gleam of danger was still far off on the horizon, but she knew it was there, throwing its harsh light over everything in anticipation. The only answer was to look away.

'Where are we going?' she asked after a while.

'Anywhere away from here.'

Safely out of Rome, he turned south and hugged the coast for about a hundred miles. There they found another beach, quiet, simple and delightfully unglamorous. The town was the same, a good place for strolling and buying toothpaste before retreating to their modest hotel and the room they shared.

'Thank goodness Sandor wasn't able to organise our accommodation this time,' Dante chuckled as they lay together in a cosy embrace late that night. 'It wasn't an accident that we were put miles apart.'

'Yes, I kind of worked that out. Low cunning.'

'Fatal mistake. I'm the master of low cunning. Someone should have warned him.'

'You're also an old-fashioned male chauvinist, now I come to think of it.'

'It took you long enough to find that out. When did you see the light?'

'You said that if I'd welcomed Sandor into my room you'd have come in and thumped him.'

'Good 'n' hard.'

'But who gave you the right to veto my lovers? What about my right to make my own choice?'

'My darling, you have an absolute right to choose any man you want.'

'Good.'

'As long as the one you choose is me.'

'And you think I'm going to put up with that nineteenth-century attitude?'

In the darkness she heard him give the rich chuckle of the triumphant male.

'Yes, because I'm not going to give you any option. Now, come here and let me make the matter plain to you.'

So she did. And he did. And after that they slept in perfect harmony.

Ferne had known from the first evening that there was more to Dante than met the eye. How many men discussed *The Divine Comedy* with a woman they'd known only a couple of hours, even if they were named after the poet?

Hope had mentioned that he had three academic degrees, and from odd remarks he dropped in their conversations she realised that this was no idle boast. His brain was agile and well-informed, and she could easily guess his horror at the thought of losing his high-powered skills.

Since she'd learned the truth about the threat to Dante's life, she'd come to see him as two men—one always standing behind the other, a permanent warning. When he was at his funniest, she was most conscious of the other man, silently threatening in the shadows, never allowing Dante to forget that he was there.

Sometimes it broke her heart that he must face his nemesis alone, and she longed to take him in her arms, not in the light-hearted passion that they usually shared, but with tender comfort. Then she remembered that he had chosen his isolation, however bitter it might be, and he wanted no comfort. Without her help, without anyone's help, he was complete and whole.

One evening he was unusually quiet, but he seemed absorbed in a book, so she'd put it down to that. Later that night she woke suddenly to find him sitting by the window, his head buried in his hands. He was completely still and silent, in such contrast to his normal liveliness that she knew a twinge of alarm.

Slipping out of bed, she went to kneel beside him.

'Is everything all right?'

'Yes, fine.' But he seemed to speak with an effort.

'You don't look well.'

'Just a bit of a headache.'

'Have you had it all evening? You haven't said much.'

'It'll go away. Just give it time.'

'Have you taken anything?'

'Yes.'

'And it doesn't work?'

'It will, in time.'

'Come back to bed. A sleep may do you good.'

'Later. Leave me now. I don't want to talk.'

'I'm only worried for you.'

'Will you drop the subject please?'

Dante's tone was light, but Ferne saw in his eyes something that reminded her of that other time. There was a steely anger, and a determination not to yield, no matter what the cost to himself or anyone else. Hastily she backed off, remembering Toni's words that to persist would be to endanger Dante, not help him.

She returned to bed, pulling the covers over her head so that she could huddle down and be alone with her thoughts. She lay awake for a long time, telling herself that this must be just an ordinary headache, the kind everyone had.

It seemed that she was right, because the next day he was his normal self. Perhaps it was only her imagination that the 'other' Dante had been there, hostile, rejecting.

One evening they bumped into Mario, an old friend from Dante's college days. The two men plunged into academic conversation, occasionally remembering their manners, apologising and drawing her in. She laughed, not at all offended, fascinated by this new angle on Dante.

When he went to fetch more drinks, Mario said, 'We all thought he'd be head of the college by now.'

'Is he really that clever?' Ferne asked.

'He could think and write rings around anyone else. I know they offered him a professorship, but he wanted to go off travelling.'

Next day she claimed tiredness, urging Dante to spend some time with Mario. He said she was the nicest, most understanding woman he'd ever known—which made her feel guilty, because she had an ulterior motive.

When she was safely alone she opened her laptop, accessed the Internet and looked up all she could find about his ailment. She had already done this once, on the day before they'd left Naples, but now she had a driving need to know far more.

A sudden bleeding into the space between the brain and an area of the lining that surrounds it; a weak blood vessel that suddenly ruptures.

Sometimes there are warning symptoms, such as headache, facial pain and double vision. This can happen minutes or weeks before the main rupture.

She read everything that she could find, forcing herself to understand every detail. The picture that kept returning to her mind was Dante going back into the burning building to rescue the dog, knowing that it might cost him his life.

When you lived with the possibility of death every moment, how much would you actually fear it? Welcome it?

There were three files that she needed to read again. Quickly she downloaded them, put them in a folder, titled it 'ZZZ', then shut everything down quickly. Finally she called Hope. Describing the headache, she said, 'I was worried at first, but he's been fine ever since, so maybe it was normal. He seems full of beans.'

'Thank you,' Hope said fervently. 'I can't tell you what it means to us to know you're with him.'

'I've got to go now. I can see him returning with his friend. I'll call again soon.'

Looking out of the window, she hailed the two men, who waved back and pointed up the street to a restaurant.

'Coming,' she called down.

It took a moment to slip the printed file into her drawer, then she was ready to leave.

The three of them spent a convivial evening, but at the end Mario seemed to forget Dante and become more interested in looking at Ferne's plunging neckline. After which, Dante said he needed an early night and swept her off to bed.

Mario departed next morning, but he left a legacy in Dante's mind. Stretched out on the beach, Ferne was startled to look up and find him doing a crossword puzzle in Latin.

'It's not difficult if you're Italian,' he demurred when she expressed her admiration. 'The two languages are so similar.'

'What's that?' she asked, pointing at a clue.

He translated for her and said, 'The answer is *quam celerrime*. It means "as quickly as possible".'

'*Quam celerrime,*' she mused. 'It has a nice, flowing sound, doesn't it? What a pity I was always useless at languages. What's the Italian version?'

'*Il più rapidamente possibile.*'

'No, I definitely prefer *quam celerrime*. Not that I could do anything with *celerrime* at the moment. I'm half-asleep.'

'Bad night?'

'No, it was a wonderful night, thank you. I just didn't get any sleep.'

He laughed, and she settled down. She was deep in happy slumber when the sound of her mobile phone reached her from a distance.

'Someone wants you,' Dante said, reaching into her bag for the phone. 'Here.'

It was a text:

Never thought you were the one to turn down the chance of a lifetime. The offer's still open and this time I want the right answer. Money, money, money. Mick.

'Who's Mick?' Dante asked, reading over her shoulder.

'Can't you tell?' Ferne asked sleepily. 'He's my sugar-daddy. He wants to cover me with diamonds and buy me an apartment in the West End, but I told him no. That stuff is old-fashioned.'

'Now I remember; he's your agent, isn't he? You mentioned him on the train the night we met.'

'Uh-huh!'

She was trying to sound half-asleep, but inside she was alert and wary. She didn't want Dante asking questions about why she'd refused a big job, in case he stumbled on the truth. Diverting him was going to be tricky.

'Why is he mad at you?' Dante asked. 'What have you turned down?'

She sighed as if it was too boring to be discussed.

'He wanted me to go back to London and do

another theatre shoot with a big star who's condescending to do a live play. Sandor Jayley with knobs on. No way!'

'Who's the star?'

She told him. Dante stared.

'You rejected *him*? Just think what you might have—'

'He's bringing his fiancée with him,' she said, trying to sound petulant. 'No chance for me to be vulgar and unprincipled there.'

Dante grinned, slipping an arm around her.

'Can I flatter myself that you prefer to be vulgar and unprincipled with me?'

'I can't stop you flattering yourself,' she observed indifferently. 'Some men are so conceited.'

'Not me. I can't believe you'd choose me over the chance to make a lot of money.'

'You forget,' she said languidly. 'I already made my fortune with Sandor.' She drew a light finger down his bare chest. 'Now I'm in the mood to spend some of it on, er, the *pleasures of the moment*.' She uttered the last words in a seductive whisper.

'Oh, really?' he said, speaking with some difficulty, she was pleased to note.

'*La grande signorina* gives her orders?'

'Definitely. And she's very demanding.'

'So I'm here only for your pleasure?'

She surveyed him with wicked glee. 'Well, what else did you imagine you were here for? I expect my every whim to be obeyed.'

'I'm your willing slave.'

'And my first whim is to swim. Into the sea with us.'

'I was hoping for something better.'

'Hmm! Being my willing slave didn't last long, did it? Come on.'

She wriggled free of him and ran down the beach, hearing him just behind her. Once in the surf, he seized her and drew her further in, until the water was up to their chests; nobody else could have seen the way his hands were wandering.

'Just what do you think you're doing?' she challenged.

'Only my duty. I wouldn't want to disappoint you.'

'But you can't do *that* in public.'

'It's not in public, it's under water. Perfectly respectable.'

'There is nothing respectable about what you're doing,' she gasped.

After that she became incapable of speech and could only cling onto him, digging her nails into his shoulder in a way that left marks for days.

When they finally returned to their loungers,

she asked him to fetch her a drink. While he was
gone she texted Mick with shaking hands.

Sorry, can't change my mind. Am out of
action for a while.

She switched off the phone and hid it away
safely, silently thanking a merciful providence
for helping her get away with it this time.

Hopefully Mick wouldn't trouble her again,
whatever he might guess.

Oh, to blazes with Mick and what he might
think! To blazes with everything, except getting
Dante back into her bed *quam celerrime*.

CHAPTER NINE

THE 'willing slave' fantasy kept them entertained for a while. Unlike many men, Dante was totally relaxed with it, his masculine confidence too powerful to be disturbed by such a joke.

They played it out in the bedroom, with her indicating her requirements and him following to the letter, both enjoying the challenge, laughing, not thinking any further. That was how they both preferred it.

One morning as they were preparing to go out the phone rang, and it was Gino.

'The film crew have left,' Dante informed Ferne when the call was over.

'Already?'

'There was some sort of a kerfuffle; Sandor threw a fit and everyone was out in an hour. Now we're needed to sell the place.' He looked at her, smiling. 'Ah, well, I guess it was too perfect to last for ever.'

'Nothing lasts for ever,' Ferne said lightly.

'That's what I say.' Then he sighed and added ruefully, 'But sometimes it would be nice if it did.'

They spent two days at the Palazzo Tirelli before heading back to Naples, where they moved into a small apartment belonging to a friend of Dante who was currently away.

On the first night back they went to dinner at the Villa Rinucci. Hope broadcast the event to the family, inviting everyone to drop in. But for her the real point of the evening was to see with her own eyes that Dante was in good health, and even better spirits.

'He's told me all about it,' she said when she and Ferne had a moment alone in the kitchen. 'You actually slapped Sandor Jayley's face because you prefer Dante?'

'I'd have slapped his face anyway,' Ferne protested. 'It had nothing to do with Dante.'

'Oh, come! What about that big offer you turned down?'

'Well, I had to, after I made you a promise. Hope, Dante and I are ships that pass in the night, we both know that. We're having fun, but it can't last. He's not in love with me, and I'm not in love with him.'

Hope didn't reply in words, but her cynical gaze was answer enough. A moment later Toni called, and they both went out to where everyone was lounging in the garden as the evening wound down.

Ferne wished she could speak openly to Hope and tell her that love was impossible because she simply wouldn't allow it to happen.

She knew she had been lucky as few women were ever lucky. Dante was a gentle and considerate man. If she was tired, he would urge her to bed, kiss her gently and either hold her until she slept or creep away, leaving her in peace.

When they talked, he listened to her with every appearance of real interest. His own conversation was fascinating. Beneath the sometimes clownish exterior was a thoughtful, educated man who might well have been a professor in some serious subject.

In bed he was a skilled and tender lover, giving her a physical pleasure she had never dreamed possible, and treating her like a queen. On the surface no woman could have asked for more.

But in her heart she had the melancholy feeling that it was all a sham, an illusion, because he was hiding the most important part of himself from her. And while that was true it would protect her from falling deeply in love with him.

She reassured herself about that many times.

Their apartment was high up on the fifth floor of a block overlooking the Bay of Naples. From their bedroom window they could see the great volcano Vesuvius in the distance. Several times she woke to find him on the window seat, contentedly watching the full moon across the bay casting its glow on the volcano.

One night he stayed up late, leaving her to come to bed alone. She'd waited for him, then fallen into a half-sleep. Somewhere in that doze she'd thought she felt a gentle kiss on her cheek, but when she opened her eyes she was alone.

She'd slept again, and had finally woken to find him sitting by the window. This was different from last time, when he'd sat with his head in his hands, clearly in pain. Now he seemed content, gazing out, still in the same thoughtful mood as before. When he saw that she was awake, he didn't speak but held out an arm for her to come and join him.

'Do you remember when we looked at this before?' he murmured.

'Yes, and you told me you'd once heard it rumble and longed to hear it again,' she said. 'There's nowhere to get away from it, is there? Wherever you are in Naples, it's always there.'

'You think you're used to it,' he murmured. 'You know it in all its phases, but you can still be taken by surprise.'

She watched him, wondering what he would

say next. He'd been in a strange mood for the last couple of days, with less to say than usual. He didn't seem sad or unwell, merely thoughtful. Occasionally she would look up to find him watching her with eyes that were almost puzzled, as though something had disconcerted him. If he caught her glance, he would smile and turn quickly away.

'What have you been taking for granted?' she asked him now.

'Everything, perhaps. You think you know how things are, but suddenly it's all different. You're not the same man you were—whoever that was.'

He gave a brief, nervous laugh, sounding mysteriously as though he had no self-confidence. 'I'm talking nonsense, aren't I?' he said.

'Mmm, but go on. It sounds good.'

'Yes, nonsense can sound very impressive. I learned that long ago. You can even impress yourself with it for a while. But—then the volcano rumbles and reminds you of things you've always known, and maybe wish you didn't.'

Ferne held her breath. Was Dante finally going to tell her the truth about himself, thus letting her come really close to him at last?

'Are you afraid of the volcano?' she whispered. 'I mean, the one inside?'

'Yes, although I wouldn't admit that to anyone but you. I've never even admitted it to myself before, but I feel I could tell you anything and it would be all right. I need never be afraid again.' He added wistfully, 'Could that ever really be true?'

'I suppose it would depend how much you wanted it to be true,' she ventured. 'If you trusted me…'

'I trust you as I've never trusted anyone in my life. If not you, then who?'

He took her hands in his, bending his head to kiss the palms.

'You have such tiny, delicate hands,' he whispered. 'Yet they're so strong, so welcoming. When they reach out, they seem to contain all the world.'

'I would give you the world if I could,' she said. It was a dangerous thing to say, but the words seemed to come out of their own accord. 'If it were mine to give.'

'Perhaps it is and you don't know it.' He stroked her face with tender fingers. 'Sometimes I think I know more about you than you know about yourself. I know how loving and honest you are, how brave, how open-hearted.'

'It's an illusion,' she said. 'That's a fantasy figure you've created.'

'Why do you say that?'

'Because nobody could be the way you see me.'

'Why? Because I think you're perfect?'

'That proves it's an illusion.'

'No, it proves I'm a man of insight and good sense. Now, don't argue with me. If I say you're perfect, you're perfect—and I do say it. I know you could never perform a deceitful or underhand action.'

His words, spoken so warmly and with such emotion, gave her a bad moment. The knowledge of her deception, however well-meaning, seemed to hang over them, poisoning the moment.

'Dante—'

His finger lightly touched her mouth. 'Don't spoil it.'

Don't spoil it. The words were like a bitter reproach.

But it wasn't her fault, she thought wildly. She was protecting him, but that innocent desire had led her up this path, fraught with danger.

'Let me say what I want to before I lose my nerve,' he murmured.

'I can't see you ever losing your nerve.'

'That's an act. Inside I'm a coward. If you only knew how much of a coward, you'd run away. And that's what you ought to do.'

'Isn't that for me to decide?'

'How can you, when you don't know the worst of me?'

'Then tell me the worst. I'm braced for anything.'

'You make a joke of it, but there are things…'

'Yes?' she said eagerly.

'Ferne…' She felt a tremor go through him. 'Have I imagined what's been happening to us?'

Now her heart was beating so hard that she couldn't speak, only shake her head.

'I know I said "just friendly",' he whispered. 'But I say a lot of things that are nonsense. I guess you know that by now. When we talk—and I've never talked to anyone the way I talk to you—I always feel that you understand everything I'm not saying. With you, I don't have to worry. I can be at peace.'

He made a wry face, aimed at himself. 'I never thought the day would come when I saw peace as a virtue. I was always one for racketing around. Yes, you knew that, didn't you?' His soft laughter joined hers. 'I don't suppose there's much about me you haven't worked out: clown, idiot, self-deceiver, overgrown schoolboy.'

'I could add a few others,' she teased.

'I'll bet you could.'

'Then how can you say I don't know the worst of you? I probably think you're worse than you are. Why don't you put me right?'

'Tell you what a hero I am? What a strong, solid, upright character who never cut corners or skirted around the truth in his life?'

'No, I don't think I could quite believe that.' She was teasing him along the road, inviting him into the place where he would feel safe enough to tell her everything. When there was total honesty between them, the way would be clear for whatever lay in the future.

She wanted there to be a future. She could admit that now. She'd hidden her feelings, even from herself, behind a barrier of caution and sensible reasoning. But now Dante himself was demolishing that barrier. If she was only a little patient, there would be happiness soon.

'It you presented yourself as a stuffed dummy full of virtue I think I'd just laugh,' she admitted. 'And then I'd send you on your way, because I'd have no use for you.'

'For the stuffed-dummy part or the virtue?' he asked lightly.

'Guess.'

He smiled, but then his smile faded as emotion swept him.

'Oh, Ferne, don't change,' he said desperately. 'Promise me you'll never change, and then maybe I can dig deep in myself and find a little courage. Only it's going to take more than just a little. It's going to take a lot to show you myself as I really am, stupid and pig-headed, blind to what matters.'

'Stop,' she said, putting her fingers lightly over his mouth. 'Don't run yourself down.'

He didn't argue, just took hold of her fingers and moved his lips against them. His eyes were almost desperate. She stroked his face, willing him to take the last step that would join their hearts in the closeness that only honesty could bring.

'Dante,' she whispered. 'Please—please.'

Suddenly he gripped her tightly, drawing her to him and burying his face against her.

'Help me,' he said huskily. *'Help me.'*

She held him eagerly, flooded with emotion that made it impossible to speak. His carefully constructed armour was cracking, revealing the vulnerability he'd striven so hard to hide, and she wanted only to enfold him, to offer him the help he'd finally sought. Now the moment had come, she was almost dizzy with joy and gratitude.

'What's this?' he said, touching her face. 'You're crying.'

'No, I'm not, not really. I'm just—'

'Don't cry.' He was lightly brushing her tears away. 'I didn't mean to upset you.'

'I'm not upset.'

He took her face between his hands, looking

down at her tenderly before dropping his mouth to hers. She kissed him back eagerly, trying to tell him silently that she was his in any way he wanted. If only they could take the next step.

'I'm so lucky to have you,' he said. 'If only…'

'If only…?' she echoed wistfully.

'If only I were worth it. There's so much I want to say to you, but not just now. My head's in a muddle—as usual,' he finished, turning it into a joke.

But she wouldn't let him get away with that.

'I don't think this is your usual muddle,' she persisted.

'No, I'm getting worse. Be a little patient with me.'

'All right,' she said, trying not to sound sad.

'Let's go to bed,' he said. 'We've got a long drive tomorrow.'

She was stunned, hardly able to believe that the emotion of a moment ago had vanished to nothing. They had come so close, and to see the prize snatched away at the last minute was hard. But she let him lead her unprotesting to bed. One incautious word from her, and the chance could be lost for ever.

He pulled the clothes up over her and got in beside her, holding her briefly before kissing her goodnight. Then he turned over and went to sleep.

She lay staring into the darkness, trying to come to terms with what had happened. It was disappointing to sense his withdrawal, yet she felt she understood. He'd meant to tell her—she was convinced—but he'd backed off, perhaps appalled by so nearly abandoning the caution of a lifetime.

Now she must be patient and it would surely happen, for there had been something in his manner that had never been there before, a new trust and tenderness. His eyes had shone with a different light, and somewhere Ferne had sensed a door opening.

How long had she loved him—right from the start? The signs had been there when he'd gone into the burning building and she, who'd coolly photographed Sandor's betrayal, had forgotten everything but Dante's danger.

She'd deceived herself, believing she was only doing this for Hope, when the truth was she yearned to be with Dante. How could she ever have imagined that it was possible to be with this man night and day and not love him?

The sadness had been to love him and hide from him, as he was hiding from her. But now that would soon be over, and she was feeling happy again as she fell asleep.

Next day they drove miles to a villa that was going to take all their joint skills to sell. But the challenge was exhilarating, and they returned home in a triumphant mood. On the drive back, Dante was in high spirits.

'We'll stop for a meal,' he said. 'But only a quick one. Let's not be late home.'

He said nothing about the day before, but there was something in the happy atmosphere that told her everything was different. He'd come to the edge of saying the words that would bind them closer, that it was almost as though they had already been said. Looking up, she saw him watching her with a contented smile that told her she was right.

When they reached home there was work to do, and they both settled down at computers.

'It's coming on really well,' he said, looking over her shoulder. 'How did I ever sell houses without you?'

'You don't have to butter me up,' she said sleepily. 'You're stuck with me, whether you want me or not.'

'That's what I like to hear. Why don't you go to bed?'

'I think I will.' She shut down her computer.

'Leave it,' Dante said. 'I'll put it away with mine.'

She kissed him and drifted away, yawning.

He watched her go, wondering if she would think it strange that tonight he didn't come to bed

with her. In fact he was hatching a plan—repre-
hensible, no doubt, but he didn't think she'd mind
too much when she found out.

She had never done as she'd promised and
emailed him the pictures he had taken of her.
Now he proposed to conduct a raid and claim
them. Waiting until he could see that she'd
turned the bedroom light off, he switched her
computer back on.

He located the folder without difficulty, and
within moments was looking at the pictures he'd
taken. He'd thought he knew them, but now they
struck him with new force. So much had
happened since then. He hadn't meant to grow so
close to her, but it had happened despite his reso-
lutions. Perhaps it was fate. He, a man who
believed in fate, had to believe in this possibility.

Now he couldn't understand why he hadn't
seen her clearly before. Entranced by her loveli-
ness, he'd overlooked the strength and honesty in
her face. It was this, as much as her passionate
body, that had broken down his defences, so that
only a day ago he'd been on the verge of telling
her things he'd never told another living soul,
things he'd sworn never to tell anyone in his life—
however long or short that life might be.

He'd come to the very edge, then backed off.
But not very far. The thought was still there in his

mind that if he plucked up courage he could tell her everything, beg her to risk the future with him. If not her, then nobody, for there was nobody else in the world that he trusted as much.

She was smiling at him from the screen, her eyes wide and clear, offering hope where there had been none before, a future where there had been only blankness.

Quickly he connected the laptop to his portable printer and printed out a copy of the picture.

That was enough for now. Tomorrow he would confess what he'd done and they would laugh together, revelling in their private world where nobody else was allowed, and where they kept each other safe.

He was about to log off when he noticed the file called 'ZZZ'.

Through her light sleep Ferne was vaguely aware of the sound of the printer coming from the next room, then a long silence, until she heard the printer again. When it ended there was another silence that dragged on and on. Without knowing why, she was suddenly filled with fear.

Moving slowly, she left the bed at the same moment that Dante entered the room. Strangely, he too was moving slowly, as though struggling to recover from some terrible blow. He switched on the light, and she saw he was holding some papers, which he tossed onto the bed. She drew a sharp breath as she recognised some of the files about his condition that she'd stored on her computer.

At the sight of Dante's face filled with cold rage, her heart nearly failed her. It was the face of a stranger.

'I printed them off your computer,' he said. 'What are they?'

'Just—something I've been reading.'

'Just something you *happened* to be reading?' His voice was calm but as cold as ice. 'I don't think so. There are at least a dozen downloads in that folder. You've been searching the Internet for anything you could find on this one subject, and you didn't just chance on it by accident, did you?' When she hesitated, he added, 'Don't lie to me, Ferne.'

If only he would return to being the Dante she knew, and not this frightening stranger. She tried to find some warmth in his eyes, but there was only a cavern of emptiness that filled her with dread.

'I won't lie to you, Dante. I knew you had a problem.'

'Who told you? Hope, I suppose?'

'Yes, she was worried about you. You had that

funny turn on the ladder the day of the fire, and then a bad headache.'

'And you both put two and two together and came up with five. I was sick with smoke that day, but you had to make a big thing of it.'

'All right, you think we were fussing about nothing, but people who care about you *do* fuss. That's how you know they care. You told me once that Hope has been the nearest thing to a mother that you've known since your own mother died. Well, mothers fuss. They may have to hide it, but it's what happens.'

'So, she told you—when? How long ago?'

'I—'

'How long ago?' he repeated relentlessly. 'Before we came away together?'

'Yes.'

'You've known all this time?' he said softly. 'There was I, like a fool, thinking I could guard my privacy, never dreaming you were spying on me.'

'I wasn't spying.'

'*This* is spying.' His voice was like the crack of a whip, making her flinch back.

'Is it wrong to care for you, to want to see you safe?'

'My safety is my own affair.'

'Not always,' she said, beginning to get angry. 'What you do affects other people. You can't spend your life cut off from everyone.' She drew a sharp breath. 'But that's what you've tried to do, isn't it?'

'That's my business.' His face was deadly pale, not white but grey. 'Is that why you came with me? As a kind of guardian, watching over me like a nurse with a child—or worse?'

'I never thought of you like that.'

'I think you did—someone so stupid that he has to be kept in the dark while he's *investigated* behind his back.'

'What did you expect me to do when you kept the truth from me?' she cried.

'*You've* been hiding secrets from *me*,' he shouted.

'I had to, but I didn't want to. I always hoped that you'd come to trust me.'

'But that's the irony; that's the ugly joke. I *did* trust you. I've never felt so close to anyone.'

'Then you were fooling yourself,' she said hotly. 'How could we be close when you were concealing something so important? That's not real closeness. That's just a pretence of it on your terms.'

'Exactly: "how could we be close when you were concealing something so important?" That says it all, doesn't it? When I think of you watching me, judging me, adjusting your actions to keep me fooled…'

He drew a sharp breath, and she saw sudden,

bitter understanding overtake him. 'That's the real reason you refused to take that job, isn't it? And there was I thinking that maybe you wanted to be with me as much as I— Well, it just shows you how a man can delude himself if he's stupid enough. I must remember to pay you back the money you sacrificed for me.'

'Don't you dare say that!' she cried. 'Don't you *dare* offer me money.'

'Do you feel insulted? Well, now you know how I feel.' His voice rose on a note of anguished bitterness. 'But can you also understand that at this moment *I can't bear the sight of you*?'

CHAPTER TEN

As IF to prove it, he turned away and began to pace the room, talking without looking at her.

'What a laugh I must have given you!'

'You don't really think that?' she said. 'You can't. I have never laughed at you.'

'Pitied, then. That's worse. Can't you understand?'

Wearily, she understood only too well. Dante was staggering under the weight of humiliation as he realised how close he'd come to opening his heart to her. For years he'd held off, never risking deep emotion and trust, until he'd met her. Now he felt betrayed.

She'd known that he guarded his privacy, but it was worse than that. He shut himself away from the world's eyes in a little cave where he dwelt alone, and even she wasn't allowed to venture. She thought of his loneliness in that bare cave, and shivered.

'I've always wanted to talk to you about it,' she said. 'I hated deceiving you. But I'd have hated it more if you'd died, and you might die if you don't have it properly checked.'

'What is there to check? I know the chances.'

'I wonder if you know as much as you think you do!' she said in a temper. 'You're a conceited man, Dante, proud, arrogant and stubborn, in a really stupid way. You think you know it all, but medical science moves on. If you'd let the doctors help you, something could be done. You could be fit and strong for years ahead.'

'You don't know what you're talking about,' he said harshly. 'Don't tell me what happens with this, because I know more about it than you ever will. I've watched what it's done to my family, the lives it's ruined; not just the people who suffer from it, but those who have to watch them die. Or, worse, when they don't die, swallowing up the lives of the people who have to care for them. Do you think I want that? Anything is better. Even dying.'

'Do you think your death would be better for me?' she whispered.

'It could be, if it set you free, if I'd made the mistake of tying you to me so that you longed for my death as much as I did.' A withered look came into his face. 'Except that I wouldn't long for it, because I wouldn't understand what was happening to me, wouldn't know. Everyone else would know, but I'd know nothing. I'd just carry on, thinking I was a normal man. *And I would rather be dead*.'

Then he stared at her in silence, as though his own words had shocked him as much as they had her. When the silence became unbearable, Ferne said bitterly, 'What about what I want? Doesn't that count?'

'How can you judge when you don't know the reality?'

'I know what my reality would be like if you died. I know it because I love you.'

He stared at her with eyes full of shock, but she searched them in vain for any sign of pleasure or welcome. This man was dead to love.

'I didn't mean to, but it happened. Did you ever think of what you were doing to me?' she pleaded.

'You weren't supposed to fall in love,' he grated. 'No complications. We were going to keep it light.'

'And you think love is like that? You think it's so easy to say "don't" and for nothing to happen? It might be easy for you. You arrange things the way you want them, you tell yourself that you'll get just so close to me and no further, and that's how things work out, because you have no real heart. But I have a heart, and I can't control it like you can.

'Yes, I love you. Dante, do you understand that? I *love* you. I am deeply, totally in love with you. I didn't want that to happen. I told myself the same silly fantasies that you did—how it could be controlled if I was sensible. And it crept up on me when I wasn't looking, and, when I did look, it was too late.

'Now I want all the things I swore I'd never let myself want: to live with you and make love with you, marry you and bear your children. I want to crack jokes with you, and hold you when you're sleeping at night.

'You never thought of that, did you? And you don't think it matters. I wish I was as heartless as you.'

'I'm not—'

'Shut up and listen. I've listened to you, now it's my turn. I wish I didn't love you, because I'm beginning to think you don't deserve to be loved, but I can't help it. So there it is. What do I do now with this love that neither of us wants?'

'Kill it,' he snapped.

'Tell me how.'

His face changed, became older, wearier, as though he had suddenly confronted a brick wall.

'There is a way,' he murmured. 'And perhaps it's the best way, if it will convince you as nothing else could.'

'Dante, what are you talking about?'

'I'm going to kill your love.'

'Even you can't do that,' she said, trying to ignore the fear that was growing inside her.

'Don't be so sure. When I'm finished, you'll recoil from me in horror and run from me as far and fast as you can. I promise you that will happen, because I'm going to make sure it does. When you look back on this time, you'll wish we'd never met, and you'll hate me. But one day you'll thank me.'

The brutal words seemed to hang in the air between them. Ferne stared at him hopelessly, vainly looking for some softening in his face.

He checked his watch. 'We have time to catch a flight if we hurry.'

'Where are we going?'

'Milan.' He gave a frightening smile. 'I'm going to show you the future.'

'I don't understand. What is there in Milan?'

'My Uncle Leo. Have they told you about him?'

'Toni said he was a permanent invalid.'

'*Invalid* doesn't begin to describe it. They say that in his youth he was a fine man, a banker with a brain like a steel trap that could solve any problem. Women basked in his attention. Now he's a man with the mind of a child.'

'I'll take your word for it. I don't need to see him.'

'I say that you do, and you're going to.'

'Dante, please listen—'

'No, the time for that is passed. Now *you* listen. You wanted me to show you how to kill your love, and that's what I'm going to do.'

She tried to twist away but his hands were hard on her shoulders.

'We're going,' he said.

'You can't make me.'

'Do you really think I can't?' he asked softly.

Who was this man who stared at her with cold eyes and delivered his orders in a brutal *staccato* that brooked no argument? Why did he have Dante's face when he wasn't Dante, could never be him?

Or was he the *real* Dante who had lived inside this man all the time?

'Go and pack your things,' he said in a voice of iron.

She did so, moving like an automaton. When she came out with her bag, he was waiting.

'The taxi will be here in a minute,' he said.

Neither spoke on the way to the airport; there was nothing to say. Ferne had the feeling of coming to a huge bridge stretching so far into the distance that she couldn't see the other side. It led to an unknown place that she feared to visit, but to turn back now was impossible.

Worst of all was the sensation of travelling there

alone, for there was no comfort to be found in the steely man beside her.

Then she caught a glimpse of his blank face, and remembered that he was the one in need of comfort. But he would accept none, especially from her.

On the flight to Milan, she ventured to say, 'What kind of place is he in?'

'A care home. It's clean, comfortable, kind. They look after him well. Sometimes his family visit him, but they lose heart after a while, because he doesn't know them.'

He added wryly, 'One strange thing that you may find useful, he still speaks excellent English. With all the damage that was done to the rest of his brain, that part has remained untouched. The doctors can't say why.'

At the airport he hailed a taxi to take them to the home, where a nurse greeted them with a smile.

'I've told him you called to say you were coming. He was so pleased.'

That sounded cheerful, Ferne thought. Perhaps Uncle Leo was better than Dante imagined.

She followed them through the pleasant building until they came to a bedroom at the back where the sun shone through large windows. A man was there, kneeling on the floor, solemnly decorating a Christmas tree. He looked up and smiled at the sight of them.

He was in his late sixties, plump and grey-haired, with twinkling eyes and an air of friendly glee.

'Hello, Leo,' said the nurse. 'Look who I've brought to see you.'

'I promised to come,' Dante said to him in English. 'And I brought a friend to see you.'

The old man smiled politely.

'How kind of you to visit me,' he said, also in English. 'But I can't talk for long. My nephew is coming, and I must get this finished.' He indicated the tree, immediately returning to work on it.

'It's his latest obsession,' the nurse said. 'He decorates it, takes it all down then starts again. Leo, it's all right, you can leave it for the moment.'

'No, no, I must finish it before Dante gets here,' Leo said urgently. 'I promised him.'

'I'm here, Uncle,' Dante said, going to him. 'There's no need to finish the tree. It's fine as it is.'

'Oh, but I must. Dante will be so disappointed otherwise. Do you know Dante, by any chance?'

Ferne held her breath, but Dante was unfazed. It seemed that he was used to this.

'Yes, I've met him,' he said. 'He's told me all about you.'

'But why doesn't he come?' Leo was almost in tears. 'He keeps saying he will, but he never does, and I so long to see him.'

'Leo, look at me.' Dante's voice was very gentle. 'Don't you know me?'

'No.' Wide-eyed, Leo stared at him. 'Should I?'

'I've often visited you before. I hoped you'd remember me.'

Leo's gaze became intense. 'No,' he said desperately. 'I've never seen you before. I don't know you—I don't, I don't!'

'It's all right, it doesn't matter.'

'Who are you?' Leo wailed. 'I don't know you. You're trying to confuse me. Go away! I want Dante. Where's Dante? He promised!'

Before their horrified eyes, he burst into violent tears, burying his face in his hands and wailing. Dante tried to take the old man in his arms but was violently pushed away. Raising his voice to a scream, Leo barged his way out of the room, racing across the lawn towards the trees.

The nurse made to follow him, but Dante waved her back. 'Leave this to me.'

He hurried out after Leo, catching up with him as they reached the trees.

'Oh dear,' Ferne sighed.

'Yes, it's very sad,' the nurse said. 'He's a sweet old man, but he gets fixated on things, like that tree, and things just go round and round in his head.'

'Is it normal for him not to recognise his family?'

'We don't see much of them here. Dante comes more often than anyone else. He's so gentle and kind to Leo. I shouldn't tell you this, but he pays the lion's share of the expenses here, plus any special treats for the old man; he gets nothing back for it.'

'And Leo has been like this for how long?'

'Thirty years. It makes you wonder how life looks from inside his head.'

'Yes,' Ferne said sadly. 'It does.'

'I suppose he doesn't really know, and that makes it bearable for him, poor thing. But then Dante visits him, and it brings him no pleasure because he never recognises him.'

Heavy-hearted, Ferne wandered out into the gardens, heading for the trees where she'd seen them go. She could understand the way Dante flinched from being reduced to this, being pitied by everyone. If only there was some way to convince him that her love was different. Inside her heart, hope was dying.

She heard them before she saw them. From somewhere beyond the trees came the sound of weeping. Following it, she came across the two men sitting on a fallen log. Dante had his arms around his uncle, who was sobbing against his shoulder.

He looked up as she approached. He said nothing, but his eyes met hers in a silent message: *now you understand. Be warned, and escape quickly.*

'Stop crying,' he said gently. 'I want you to meet a friend of mine. You can't cry when a lady is here—she'll think you don't like her.'

The gentle rallying in his voice had its effect. Leo blew his nose and tried to brighten up.

'Buon giorno, signorina.'

'No, no, my friend is English,' Dante said. 'We must speak English to her. She doesn't understand foreign languages as we do.' He emphasised 'we' very slightly, clearly trying to create a sense of closeness that would comfort Leo. 'Her name is Ferne Edmunds.'

Leo pulled himself together. 'Good evening, Miss Edmunds.'

'Please, call me Ferne,' she said. 'I'm so glad to meet you.' Floundering for something to say, she looked around at the trees. 'This is a lovely place.'

'Yes, I've always liked it. Of course,' Leo added earnestly, 'it's a lot of work to keep it in good condition. But it's been in my family for such a long time, I feel I must—I must—' He broke off, looking around in bewilderment.

'Don't worry about it,' Dante said, taking his hand and speaking quietly. 'It's all being taken care of.'

'I so much wanted everything to be right when he came,' Leo said sadly. 'But he isn't coming, is he?'

'Leo, it's me,' Dante said urgently. 'Look at me. Don't you recognise me?'

For a long moment Leo gazed into Dante's face, his expression a mixture of eagerness and sadness. Ferne found herself holding her breath for both of them.

'Do I know you?' Leo asked sadly after a while. 'Sometimes I think—but he never comes to see me. I wish he would. He said once that he was the only person who really understood me, and he'd always be my best friend. But he doesn't visit me, and I'm so sad.'

'But I do visit you,' Dante said. 'Don't you remember me?'

'Oh no,' Leo sighed. 'I've never seen you before. Do you know Dante?'

At first she thought Dante wouldn't answer. His head was bowed as though some terrible struggle was taking place within him, consuming all his strength. At last he managed to say, 'Yes, I know him.'

'Please, please ask him to come to see me. I miss him so much.'

Dante's face was full of tragedy, and Ferne's heart ached for him. He'd been right; the reality was more terrible than anything she could have imagined.

'Let's go back inside,' he said, helping Leo to his feet.

In silence they made their way back across the lawn. Leo had recovered his spirits, as if the last few minutes had never been, and was chatting happily about the grand estate he believed was his.

The nurse came out onto the step, smiling kindly at Leo, welcoming him inside.

'We've got your favourite cakes,' she said.

'Oh, thank you. I've been trying to explain to my friend here about Dante. Look, let me show you his picture.'

From a chest of drawers behind the bed Leo took a photo album and opened it at a page containing one picture. It was Dante, taken recently. He was sitting with Leo, both of them smiling and seeming content with each other. Leo looked at it with pride.

'That was taken— Well, you can see that he's nothing like…' He looked at Dante sorrowfully.

Ferne felt her throat constrict and knew that in another moment she would be weeping. The picture was clearly Dante, and the fact that Leo didn't recognise him told a terrible story about his mental state.

'You see what a nice boy he is,' Leo said, running his fingers over the face on the page. 'He was always my favourite. Look.'

He began turning the pages, revealing earlier pictures. Ferne gasped as she saw Leo as a young man before his tragedy, sitting with a little boy on his knee. Even at this distance of years she could recognise Dante in the child. His face was the one she knew, bright and vivid with intelligence, gleaming with humour.

But the greatest tragedy of all was the fact that the man's face was exactly the same. Their features were different, but their expressions were identical. In his day, Leo had been the man Dante was now, dazzling, charmingly wicked, capable of anything.

And he had come to this.

Turning the pages, Leo revealed more pictures, including one of a beautiful young woman.

'That was my wife,' he said softly. 'She died.'

But Dante shook his head, mouthing, 'Left him.'

There was the child Dante again, with a man and a woman.

'My sister Anna,' Leo said proudly. 'And her husband, Taddeo Rinucci. They died in a car accident years ago.'

He switched back to the modern picture of Dante and showed it to the real man.

'You see? If you could remember what he looks like, and then—?' Tears began to roll down his face.

Ferne's heart broke for Dante, sitting there regarding this tragedy with calm eyes. When he spoke to Leo, it was with tender kindness, asking nothing, giving everything.

'I'll remember,' he said. 'Trust me for that. And I'll try to find some way of making things nicer for you. You know you can rely on me.'

'Oh yes,' Leo said brightly. 'You're always so good to me—who are you?'

'It doesn't matter,' Dante said with an effort. 'As long as we're friends, names don't matter.'

Leo beamed.

'Oh, thank you, thank you. I want—I want—'

Suddenly he was breathing wildly and shuddering. His arms began to flail, and it took all Dante's strength to hold him in his chair.

'You'd better go,' the nurse said tersely. 'We know what to do when he's like this.'

'I'll call later,' Dante said.

'By all means, but please go now.'

Reluctantly they did so.

'What happened to him?' Ferne asked as they left.

'He had an epileptic seizure,' Dante said bluntly. 'That's another thing that happens with his condition. He'll lose consciousness, and when he awakens he won't remember anything, even our visit. Once this happened and I insisted on staying, but my presence only distressed him. Possibly it's my fault he had the seizure, because seeing me agitated him.'

'That poor man,' she said fervently.

'Yes, he is. And, now you know, let's go to the airport. You've seen all you need to.'

She agreed without argument, sensing that Dante was at the end of his tether.

They spoke little on the short flight back to Naples. Ferne felt as though she never wanted to speak another word again. Her mind seemed to be filled with darkness, and she could see only more darkness ahead. Perhaps things would be better when they got home and could talk about it. She tried hard to believe that.

But, when they reached home, he stopped at the front door.

'I'm going for a walk,' he said. 'I'll be back later.'

She knew better than to suggest coming with him. He wanted to get away from her; that was the truth.

And perhaps, she thought as she opened the front door, she too needed to be away from him for a while. That was the point they had reached.

The apartment was frighteningly quiet. She'd been alone there before, but the silence hadn't had this menacing quality because Dante's laughing spirit had always seemed to be with her, even when he was away. But now the laughter was dead, perhaps for ever, replaced by the hostility of a man who felt he'd found betrayal where he'd thought to find only trust.

It had all happened so fast. Only hours ago,

she'd been basking in the conviction of his unspoken love, certain that the trouble between them could be resolved and the way made clear. Then the heavens had fallen on her.

No, on them both. Even when Dante had been at his most cruel, she had recognised the pain and disillusion that drove him. Her heart cried that he should trust her, but life had taught him that the traps were always waiting at his feet, ready to be sprung when he least expected it.

In desperation she'd told him that she loved him, but now it hit her with the force of a sledge-hammer that he hadn't said as much in return. He'd spoken only of killing her love, and had done his best to do it. With all her heart she longed to believe that he'd been forcing himself, denying his true feelings, but she was no longer sure what those feelings were. At times, she'd thought she detected real hatred in his eyes.

Perhaps that was the real Dante, a man whose need to keep the world at bay was greater than any love he could feel. Perhaps the cold hostility he'd turned on her was the strongest emotion he could truly feel.

She sat there in the darkness, shaking with misery and despair.

In the early hours she heard him arrive, moving

quietly. When the door of the bedroom opened just a little, she said, 'I'm awake.'

'I'm sorry, did I wake you?' His voice was quiet.

'I can't sleep.'

He didn't come near the bed but went to stand by the window, looking out in the direction of Vesuvius, as they had once done together.

'That was what you meant, wasn't it?' she asked, coming beside him. 'Never knowing when it was going to send out a warning.'

'Yes, that was what I meant.'

'And, now that it has, we're all supposed to make a run for it?'

'If you have any sense.'

'I never had any sense.'

'I know.' He gave a brief laugh. 'Nobody who knew us would imagine I was the one with common sense, would they?'

'Certainly not me,' she said, trying to recapture their old bantering way of talking.

'So I have to be wise for both of us. I should think what happened today would have opened your eyes. You saw what's probably waiting for me at the end of the road.'

'Not if you take medical help to avoid it,' she pressed.

'There is no avoiding it, or at least so little

chance as not to justify the risk. To become like Leo is my nightmare. Maybe one day it'll happen, and if we were married what would you do? Would you have the sense to leave me then?'

Ferne stared at him, unable to believe that he'd really spoken such words.

'You'd want me to leave you—just abandon you?'

'I'd want you to get as far away from me as possible. I'd want you to go where you'd never have to see me, or even think about me, again.'

Shattered, Ferne stepped back and looked at him. Then a blind rage swept over her and she drew back her hand, ready to aim at his face, but at the last minute she dropped it and turned away, almost running in her fear of what she had been about to do.

He came after her, also furious, pulling her around to face him.

'If you want to hit me, do it,' he snapped.

'I ought to,' she breathed.

'Yes, you ought to. I've insulted you, haven't I? Fine, I'll insult you again. And again. Until you face reality.'

The rage in his voice frightened her. Part of her understood that his cruelty was a deliberate attempt to drive her off her for own sake. Yet still it stunned her in its intensity, warning her of depths to him that she had never understood because he had never wanted her to understand.

'Reality means what you want it to mean,' she said. 'Maybe I see things differently.'

'Marriage? Children? Holding hands as we wander into the sunset? Only I wouldn't just be holding your hand, I'd be clinging to it for support.'

'And I'd be glad to give you that support, because I love you.'

'Don't love me,' he said savagely. 'I have no love to give back.'

'Is that really true?' she whispered.

The look he gave her was terrible, full of despair and suffering that she could do nothing to ease. That was when she faced the truth: if she had no power to ease his pain, then everything was dead between them.

'Try not to hate me,' he said wearily.

'I thought you wanted me to hate you as the quickest way of getting rid of me.'

'I thought so too, but I guess I can't manage it. Don't hate me more than you have to, and I'll try not to hate you.'

'Hate *me*?' she echoed. 'After everything we've— Could you hate me?'

He was silent for a long moment before whispering, 'Yes. If I must.'

He looked away again, out of the window, to

where the dawn was breaking. The air was clear and fresh; the birds were beginning to sing. It was going to be a glorious day.

She came up close behind him, touching him gently and resting her cheek against his back. Her head was whirling with the words that she wanted to say, and yet no words would be enough.

She could feel him warm against her, as she'd known him so often before, and suddenly, irrationally, she was filled with hope. This was Dante, who loved her, no matter what he said. They would be together because it was fated. All she had to do was convince him of that.

'Darling,' she whispered.

His voice was hard, and he spoke without looking at her.

'There's a flight to England at eleven this morning. I've booked your seat.'

He came with her to the airport, helping her to check in and remaining with her as they waited for the first call. There was no more tenderness in his manner than there had been before. He was doing his polite duty.

She couldn't bear it. Whatever might happen, there was no way she could go one way and leave him to go another, at the mercy of any wind that blew.

'Dante, please.'

'Don't.'

'Tell me to stay,' she whispered. 'We'll make it work somehow.'

He shook his head, his eyes weary and defeated. 'It's not your fault. It's me. I can't change. I'll always be a nightmare for any woman to live with. You were right. I shouldn't have lived with you and not warned you. I made the terms but didn't tell you what they were. Doesn't that prove I'm a monster?'

'You're not a monster,' she said fervently. 'Just a man trapped in a vicious web. But you don't have to live in it alone. Let me come inside, let me help you.'

His face was suddenly wild.

'And see you trapped too? No, get out while you can. I've done you so much damage, I won't do more. For pity's sake, for *my* sake, go!'

He almost ran from her then, hurrying into the crowd without looking back even once. She watched as the distance between them grew wider, until he vanished.

But only from her sight. In her mind and heart where he would always live, she could still see him, making his way back to the empty apartment and the empty life, where he would be alone for ever in the doubly bitter loneliness of those who had chosen their isolation.

CHAPTER ELEVEN

IT WAS late at night when Ferne reached her apartment, to find it gloomy and cold. Locking the door behind her, she stood in the silence, thinking of Dante far away, locked in a chill darkness that was more than physical.

She'd eaten nothing all day, and after turning on the heating she began to prepare a meal, but suddenly she stopped and simply went to bed. She had no energy to be sensible.

Where are you? she thought. *What are you doing? Are you lying alone, your thoughts reaching out to me, as mine to you? Or are you passing the time with some girl you picked up for the evening? No, it's too soon. You'll do that eventually, but not just yet.*

She slept for a little while, awoke, slept again. Sleeping or waking, there were only shadows in all directions. At last she was forced to admit that a new day had dawned, and slowly got out of bed.

Her first action was to call Hope. She'd managed to keep her up to date about the disaster, Dante's discovery of her files, their trip to Milan and her return to England, and Hope had asked for a call to say she'd arrived safely.

'I meant to call last night, but I got in so late,' she apologised.

'Never mind. How are you? You sound terrible.'

'I'll be fine when I've had a cup of tea,' she said, trying to sound relaxed.

'How are you really?' Hope persisted with motherly concern.

'I'll need a little time,' she admitted. 'How's Dante?'

'He'll need time too. Carlo and Ruggiero went round to see him last night. He wasn't at home, so they trawled the local bars until they found him sitting in a corner, drinking whisky. They took him home, put him to bed and stayed with him until morning. Carlo just called me to say he's awake, with an almighty hangover, but otherwise all right.'

They parted with mutual expressions of affection. A few minutes later the phone rang. It was Mike.

'I've been hearing rumours,' he said. 'They say you might be back in the land of the living.'

She almost laughed. 'That's one way of putting it. I'm back in England.'

'Great! I have work piling up for you.'

'I thought you dumped me.'

'I don't dump people with your earning potential. That job you turned down is still open. They tried someone else, didn't like the result and told me to get you at any price. It's fantastic money.'

The money was awesome. If the Sandor episode had propelled her into the big time, her refusal of an even better offer had given her rarity value.

'All right,' she interrupted Mike at last. 'Just tell me when and where, and I'll be there.'

Later that day she went to the theatre, where the major star and his equally famous fiancée were rehearsing. From the first moment everything went well. They liked her, she liked them. Their genuine love for each other made them, at least for the moment, really nice people. They praised her pictures and insisted that she must take some more at their wedding.

The tale of her meeting with Sandor in Italy had got out. She began to receive offers to 'tell all' to the press. She refused them, but Sandor had heard rumours and become nervous, having given a self-serving interview to a newspaper, illustrated with several of Ferne's notorious pictures. Her fame had increased. So had her price.

All around her, life was blossoming.

No, she thought, not life. Just her career. Life no longer existed.

She talked regularly with Hope and gained the impression that Dante's existence was much like her own, outwardly successful but inwardly bleak.

But there was no direct word from him until she'd been home for a month, and then she received a text:

> Your success is in all the papers. I'm glad you didn't lose out. Dante.

She texted back:

> I lost more than you'll ever know.

After that there was silence. Desperately she struggled to reconcile herself to the fact that she would never hear from him again, but then she received a letter.

> I know how generous you are, and so I dare to hope that in time you will forgive me for the things I said and did. Yes, I love you; I know that I shall always love you. But for both our sakes I can never tell you again.

Night after night she wept with the letter pressed against her heart. At last she replied:

You don't need to tell me again. It's enough that you said it once. Goodbye, my dearest.

He didn't reply. She had not expected him to.

Her sleep was haunted by wretched dreams. In one she found that time had passed and suddenly there he was, older but still Dante. She reached out eagerly to him but he only gazed at her without recognition. Someone took him by the arm to lead him away.

Then she knew that the worst had happened, and he'd become the brain-damaged man he'd always feared. She longed for him to look back at her just for a moment, but he never did. She'd been blotted from his mind as if she had never been.

She woke from that dream to find herself screaming.

Struggling up in bed, she sat fighting back her sobs until suddenly her whole body seemed to become one gigantic heave. She flung herself out of bed and just managed to dash to the bathroom in time.

When it was over, she sat shivering and considering the implications.

It could be just a tummy bug, she thought. *It doesn't mean I'm pregnant.*

* * *

But it did. And she knew it. A hurried visit to the chemist, and a test confirmed it.

The discovery that she was to have Dante's child came like a thunderclap. She'd thought herself modern, careful, sensible, but in the dizzying delight of loving him she'd forgotten everything else. In a moment her life had been turned upside down. Everything she'd considered settled was in chaos.

A child of Dante's, born from their love, but also born with chance of the hereditary illness that had distorted his life: a constant reminder of what she might have had and had lost.

The sensible answer was a termination, but she dismissed the thought at once. If she couldn't have Dante, she could still have a little part of him, and nothing on earth would persuade her to destroy that. Fiercely she laid her hands over her stomach, still perfectly flat.

'I won't let anyone or anything hurt you,' she vowed. 'No matter what the future holds, you're mine, and I'll keep you safe.'

Then she realised that she'd spoken the words aloud, and looked around the apartment, wondering who she'd really been addressing. One thing was for sure: Dante had a right to know, and then, perhaps…

'No, no!' she cried. 'No false hopes. No fantastic dreams. Just tell him and then—and then?'

Once her mind was made up, she acted quickly,

calling Mike and clearing the decks at work. Then she got on a plane to Naples, and booked into a hotel. She told nobody that she was coming, not even Hope. This was between Dante and herself.

It was still light when she walked the short distance to the apartment block and stood looking up at his windows, trying to discern any sign of life. But it was too soon for lamps to be on.

She took the lift to the fifth floor and hesitated. It was unlike her to lack confidence, but this was so vital, and the next few minutes so important. She listened, but could hear nothing from inside. The silence seemed a bleak forecast of what was to come. Suddenly her courage drained away and she stepped back.

But her spirit rebelled at the thought of giving up without trying, and she raised her hand to ring the bell. Then she dropped it again. What was the point? Dante himself had believed that you couldn't buck fate, and now she saw that he was right. Fate was against them. Defeated, she headed for the elevator.

'Don't go!'

The words were almost a scream. Turning, she saw Dante standing there in his doorway. His hair was dishevelled, his shirt torn open, his face was haggard and his eyes looked as though he hadn't slept for a month. But the only thing she noticed was that his arms were outstretched to her, and the next moment she was enfolded in them.

They held each other in silence, clasped tight, not kissing, but clinging to each other as if for refuge.

'I thought you were never going to knock,' he said frantically. 'I've been waiting for you.'

'You knew I was coming?'

'I saw you standing down there. I didn't believe it at first. I've seen you so often and you always vanished. Then I heard the lift coming up, and your footsteps—but you didn't ring the bell, and I was afraid it was just another hallucination. I've had so many; I couldn't bear another. So many times you've come to me and vanished before I could wake and keep you here.'

He drew her into the apartment, and enfolded her in his arms again.

'Thank God you're here,' he said, words that carried her to the heights.

But his next words dashed her down again.

'I've longed to see you just once more. We parted badly, and it was my fault. Now at least there can be peace between us.'

So in that he hadn't changed. He was no longer denying his love, but in the long term he was still determined to keep apart from her.

She took a deep breath. Relief at finding him

here had undermined her resolution, but now the moment had arrived.

'It isn't that simple,' she said, stepping back and regarding him with loving eyes. 'Something's happened. I came to tell you about it—but then I'll go away if you like, and you need never see me again.'

His mouth twisted. 'That doesn't work very well.'

'No, with me neither, but when you hear what I have to say you might be so angry that you want me to leave.'

'Nothing could make me angry with you.'

'You were once.'

'I stopped being angry a long time ago. Most of it was aimed at myself. I forced you into an impossible situation, I know that. I should have stayed clear of you from the start.'

'It's too late for that. The time we had together has left me with more than memories.' Seeing him frown, she said, 'I'm going to have a baby, Dante.'

Just for a moment she saw joy on his face, but it was gone in an instant, as though he'd quenched it forcibly.

'Are you sure?' he breathed.

'There's no doubt. I did a test, and then I came here to tell you, because you have the right to know. But that's it. I don't expect you to react in a conventional way because I know you can't.'

'Wait, wait!' he said fiercely. 'I need time to take this in. You can't just— A baby! Dear God!'

'I did dare to hope you'd be pleased,' she said sadly. 'But I suppose you can't be.'

'Pleased—at bringing another child into the world to spend a lifetime wondering what was happening inside him? I thought we were safe, that you were taking care; hell, I don't know what I thought. But I always swore I'd never father a child.'

'Well, you've fathered one,' she said quietly. 'We have to go on from there. You can't turn the clock back.'

'There is one way.'

'No,' she said firmly. 'Don't even mention that. If you think for a moment that I could destroy your child, you don't begin to know me. I told you I love you, but I could easily hate you if you ask me to do that.'

But she couldn't stay angry as she looked at him, saddened by the confusion in his face. He'd always insisted on being in control, quick-stepping with fate to the edge, but now he'd reached an edge he'd never dreamed of and he was lost. The thought gave her an idea.

'Fate doesn't always do what we expect,' she said, slipping her arms about his neck. 'It's had this waiting for you quite a while, and it's probably been laughing up its sleeve, thinking it's found the way to defeat you. But we're not going to let it win.'

He rested his forehead against hers. 'Doesn't fate always win?' he whispered.

'That depends who you have fighting with you.' She stepped back, taking his hand and laying it over her stomach. 'You're not alone any more. There are two of us backing you up now.'

He stared. 'Two?'

'Two people fighting on your side.' She gave a faint smile at the stunned look on his face, and pointed to her stomach. 'There is actually someone in there, you know. A person. I don't know if it's a boy or a girl, but it's yours, and it's as ready to defend you as I am. When you get to know each other, you'll be the best of friends.'

He was very still, and she sensed him holding his breath as he struggled to come to terms with ideas that had always been alien to him.

'It won't be easy,' she urged, speaking with gentle persistence. 'It may have your family's inherited illness, so we'll find out, and if the news is bad at least you'll be there to help. You can explain things that nobody else can. The two of you will probably form an exclusive society that shuts me out, but I won't mind, because you'll have each other, and that's all you'll really need.'

'No,' he said softly. 'Never shutting you out, because we can't manage without you. But, my love, you don't know what you're letting yourself in for.'

'Yes, I do: a life of worry, always wondering how long the happiness will last.'

'If you know that—'

'But the other choice is a life without you, and I choose you. I choose you for me and as a father for our child, because nobody else can be the father you can. Nobody else knows the secrets you do.'

He held her close, where she belonged, where she'd dreamed of being all the long, lonely weeks. They neither kissed nor caressed, but stood still and silent, rediscovering each other's warmth, coming home. At last he led her into the bedroom and drew her down onto the bed.

'Don't worry,' he said quickly. 'I won't try to make love to you.'

'Darling, it's all right,' she said shakily. 'I'm in the early stages. It's quite safe.'

'Safe,' he whispered. 'What does "safe" mean? You can never be sure, can you? And we won't take any risks.' He gave a sharp, self-critical laugh. 'Listen to me, talking about not taking risks. But I'm such a selfish beggar; I've never had to think about anyone else's health before. I guess I'll have to get working on that.'

She kissed him in a passion of tenderness.

'You're almost there now,' she murmured.

'Almost?'

'There's something I want you to do,' she said, speaking quietly, although her heart was beating hard. 'We're going to find out the truth about your condition. I can't live with the uncertainty.'

'And if the worst is true?' he asked slowly.

'Then we'll face it. Not just for our sake, but for our child's too. This is your baby, born into the same heritage, and I want to know what it may face. If I don't know the truth, I shall worry myself sick, and that isn't a good thing for the baby. Do this for me, my love.'

In the long silence she sensed his agony and enfolded him protectively, trying to speak of her love without words.

'Be a little patient,' he begged at last. 'Don't ask me just yet.'

She understood. She was asking him to overturn the rules on which his whole life had been lived, and it was hard. All his major decisions had been taken alone. Now she'd told him that he had two supporters, but he was still struggling to adjust to that idea, or even understand it.

'Take your time,' she whispered.

They slept without making love, and when she woke at first light it was no surprise to find him sitting by the window, as he had often done before. She went to join him, sitting quietly. He didn't turn his head, but his fingers entwined with hers.

'It's still waiting there,' he said, indicating the silent volcano. 'I guess it finally gave me the rumble I wasn't prepared for. And, as I always feared, I have no answer. Why don't you despise me, run a mile, kick me out of your life?'

'Because without you I'd get bored,' she said, with a note of their old teasing. 'And, when our child asks where Daddy is, what do I tell her?'

'Say you chucked him out with the rest of the rubbish. Or you might recycle me into a sensible man.'

'Then how would I know it was you?' she asked with a hint of a chuckle.

'And what's this *her* business? Since when did she become a girl?'

'I've decided it's going to be a girl. We're better at being practical.'

He cocked a humorous eyebrow. 'I need another woman nagging me?'

'That's definitely what you need. Hope and I aren't enough. It's a task for three.'

Then her smile faded as she saw something on a nearby table and reached out for it. 'That's one of the pictures you took of me when I first came here.'

'We went to the consulate to get you a new passport,' he recalled.

'But how do you come to have it? I never did remember to give them to you.'

'No, and I raided your computer for them. This was the best, so I printed it out to keep.' He stopped and watched her for a moment, remembering. 'I'd never loved you as much as I did then. That previous night, I came to the edge of telling you everything.

'I backed off at the last minute, but when I went through those pictures and saw how you looked at me I knew I had to tell you, because you were the only person I could ever trust with the truth. Suddenly it was all clear, and I knew I could tell you everything.'

'Oh no,' she whispered, dropping her head into her hands. 'And then you found that folder and realised I'd betrayed you. No wonder you were so terribly hurt.'

'You didn't betray me. I've known that for a long time, but I was in such a state of confusion that I couldn't wait to be rid of you. You made me think, and I didn't want to think. It was only after you'd gone that I realised what I'd done—chosen safety and predictability over life. I kept that picture with me to remind myself what I'd lost.'

'But why didn't you call me and ask me to come back?' she asked.

'Because I thought I had nothing to offer you, and you were better without me.'

'That will never be true. I want you with me all my life.'

'If only…' he said longingly.

'My love, I know what I'm asking of you is hard, but do it for me. Do it for *us*.'

Without speaking, he slipped to his knees and laid his face against her, his hand gently touching her stomach. Ferne caressed him, also in silence. Nothing more was needed. He had given his answer.

Hope was in ecstasies as they reached the villa that evening, greeting them both, but especially Ferne, with open arms.

'Welcome to the family,' she said. 'Oh yes, you're a Rinucci now. You're going to have a Rinucci baby, and that makes you one of us.'

Ferne couldn't help smiling at the way she'd been taken over. Then Hope went even further.

'I'm so looking forward to another grandchild,' she said blissfully.

'But Dante isn't actually your son, is he?' Ferne said, startled.

'Oh, son, nephew, what does it matter? He's a Rinucci, and now so are you.'

Next day, she took over the preparations for Dante's tests, telephoning a contact at the local hospital. He moved fast, and Dante was admitted that day for a lumbar puncture and a CT scan. From behind a window, Ferne watched as he prepared for the scan; he kept his eyes on them until the last minute, as he was swallowed up in the huge machine.

After that the minutes seemed to go at a crawl until they were given the results. During that endless time, Ferne realised that she had always known what the truth would be.

'The tests show that you've already had one mild rupture quite recently,' the doctor said. 'You were lucky. You came through it. You might even go on being lucky. Or you could have a major rupture in a few weeks and possibly die.'

Dante didn't reply, but sat in terrible stillness, as though already dead. After a lifetime of avoiding this moment, he was forced to confront it.

'But surgery can make it all right?' Ferne's voice was almost pleading.

'I wish I could say that it was as simple as that,' the doctor replied. 'The operation is very difficult, and there's a high death-rate. But if he goes into a coma first then the rate is even higher.' He addressed Dante directly. 'Your best chance is to have it now before things get worse.'

Dante had been sitting with head sunk in hands. Now he looked up.

'And if I live,' he said, 'can you guarantee that I'll still be mentally normal?' He choked into silence.

Gravely the doctor shook his head.

'There's always a chance of complications,' he said. 'I wish I could give you a guarantee, but I can't.'

He walked out, leaving them alone, holding each other in silence. After all the dancing with fate, all the arguments, there was only the bleak reality left. With the operation or without it, the possibility of death was high. And, with it, there was a real chance of something Dante considered far worse.

Why should he choose to walk into the unknown? Ferne knew that there was only their love to make the risk worthwhile, but was that enough? Now he was really dancing to the edge of the abyss, but not with fate, with herself, trusting her to stop him plunging over. But even she had no power to do that.

At that moment she would not have blamed him for walking away.

'What am I going to do?' he asked desperately. 'Once I would have said that dying didn't worry me, and it would have been true. But now there's you—and her.' He pointed downwards, and a wry smile twisted his mouth. 'Who'd have thought that having something to live for could be so scary?'

She waited for him to say more. The only words that mattered would come from him.

'I've used my illness as a way of avoiding responsibility,' he said after a while. 'I didn't see it like that at the time. I thought I was doing the sensible thing. Now it just looks like a form of cowardice. My whole life has been a sham because I couldn't face the reality.'

He looked at her in agony, whispering fiercely, 'Where do you get your courage? Can't you give some to me? Because I don't have any. Part of me still says just walk away and let it happen as it will.'

'No!' she said fiercely. 'I need you with me. You've got to take every chance of staying alive.'

'Even if it means becoming like Leo? That scares me more than dying.'

She drew back and looked into his face.

'Listen to me. You ask me to give you courage, but can't you understand that I need *you* to give *me* courage?'

'Me? A clown, a chancer?'

'Yes, a clown, because I need you and your silly jokes to shield me from the rest of the world. I need you to make fun of me and trip me up, and take me by surprise and get the world in proportion for me. You made me strong and whole, so that now I need to be able to reach out and hold your hand for *my* protection, not yours.'

He searched her face intently, trying to discern the answer to mysteries. At last he seemed to find what he needed, for he drew her close, resting his head on her shoulder.

'I'll do whatever you wish,' he said. 'Only promise to be there.'

CHAPTER TWELVE

THE doctor emphasised that there was no time to lose, and a date was set for the next day.

They spent that evening at the villa, where the family had gathered to wish Dante well. He had apparently recovered his spirits, even making a joke of his new deference to Ferne.

'I don't believe this is Dante,' she said. 'It's so unlike him to keep agreeing with me.'

'He's turning into a Rinucci husband,' Toni said. 'However strong we look to the rest of the world, at home we all obey orders.'

Nobody knew which of the wives murmured, 'So I should hope,' but the others all nodded agreement, and the husbands grinned.

'But he's not a husband,' Hope pointed out. 'Perhaps it's time that he was.'

'You'll have to ask Ferne,' Dante said at once. He smiled up at her with a hint of the old, wicked humour. 'I just do as I'm told.'

'Then you'll be a perfect Rinucci husband,' she said in a shaking voice.

'But when is the wedding?' Hope asked.

'As soon as I come out of hospital,' Dante said.

'No,' Hope said urgently. 'Don't wait so long. Do it now.'

Everyone knew what she meant. It might be now or never.

'Can it be arranged so quickly?' Ferne asked.

'Leave it with me,' Hope said.

She had contacts all over Naples, and it was no surprise when after a few phone calls she announced that an emergency service could be arranged for the next day. The wedding would be in the afternoon, and Dante would enter the hospital straight afterwards.

It was all achieved in double-quick time, and Ferne was left worried that Dante felt he was being hustled into marriage. Her fear increased when he was quiet on the way home.

'Dante?'

'Hush, don't speak until you've heard what I have to say. Wait here.'

He went into the bedroom and searched a drawer, returning a few moments later with two small boxes. Inside one, Ferne saw two wedding-rings, large and small. Inside the other was an engagement ring of diamonds and sapphires.

'They belonged to my parents,' he said, taking out the engagement ring. 'I never thought the day would come when I'd give this to any woman. But then, you're not any woman. You're the one I've been waiting for all this time.'

He slipped it onto her finger, dropped his head and kissed the spot. Ferne couldn't speak. She was weeping.

'And these,' he said, turning to the other box, 'are the rings they exchanged on their wedding day. They loved each other very much. He got up to mad tricks, and she tried to stick with him whenever she could. She was afraid that he'd vanish without her.

'I used to blame her for that. I felt resentful that she took risks without thinking of me, left behind. But I understand now. I've come to understand a lot of things that were hidden from me before.'

His voice shook so much that he could barely say the last words. He bent his head quickly, but not quickly enough to hide the fact that his cheeks were wet. Ferne held him tightly, fiercely glad that in her arms he felt free to weep, and that she too had come to understand many things.

That night they made love as if for the first time. He touched her gently, as though afraid to do her harm. She responded to him with passionate tenderness, and always the thought lay between them: perhaps never again; perhaps this was all there would be to last a lifetime. When their love-making was over, they held each other tenderly.

Next morning a lawyer called with papers for Dante to sign, and also some for Ferne.

'They're in Italian. I don't understand a word,' she said.

'Just sign them,' he told her. 'If I become unable to manage my own affairs, this will give you complete control.'

She was a little puzzled, since surely as his wife her control would be automatic? But perhaps Italian law was more complicated. She signed briefly, and returned to her preparations.

There was no lavish bridal-gown, just a silk, peach-coloured dress that she already knew he liked. In a dark, formal suit, he looked as handsome as she'd ever seen him. Standing side by side, looking in the mirror together, they made a handsome couple.

Both of them tried not to look at the suitcase he would take with him, which contained his things so that he could go on to the hospital when the wedding was over.

At last the lawyer departed and they were alone, waiting for the taxi.

'I think it's here,' she said, looking out of the window. 'Let's go.'

'Just a moment.' He detained her.

'What is it?'

'Just one more thing I have to know before we go ahead,' he said quietly. 'I want to marry you more than anything on earth, but I can't face the thought of being a burden in your life. Will you give me your word to put me in a home if I become like Uncle Leo?'

'How can I do that?' she asked, aghast. 'It would be a betrayal.'

'I can't marry you to become a burden on you. If you don't give me your word, the wedding's off.'

'Dante…'

'Understand me, I mean it. One way or another, I'll leave you free.'

'And your child?'

'We just signed papers that will give you complete control, whether we're married or not. So you'll have everything that's mine to support you and our child.'

'Did you think I was talking about money?' she asked with a touch of anger.

'No, I know you weren't, but you have to know that my arrangements will look after you both, even without a wedding.'

She sighed. Even now he was setting her at a little distance.

'Do I have your word,' he asked again, 'that if I become *incapable*…?' He shuddered.

'Hush,' she said, unable to endure any more.

'I don't want people to see me and pity me. I don't want my child to grow up regarding me with contempt. Do I have your word that if this goes wrong you'll put me away?' He took her hand in his. 'Swear it, or I can't marry you.'

'*What?*' She stared, appalled at this unsuspected ruthlessness.

'I'll call it off right now if you don't give me your word. I can't go through with it unless I'm sure. You've never really understood what that dread means to me, have you? And I've never been able to make you.'

'I know it means more to you than I do!' she said wildly.

This should have been their most perfect moment, when they could be happy in their love despite all the problems. But she was saddened at his intransigence.

Perhaps he saw this, because his voice became gentler.

'Nothing means more to me than you,' he said. 'But try to understand, my love; you've done so much for me. I beg you to do this one thing more, to give me peace.'

'All right,' she said sadly. 'I swear it.'

'Promise on everything you hold dear and sacred, on the life of our child, on whatever love you have for me—*promise me.*'

'I promise. If it comes to that—' she paused, and a tremor went through her '—I'll do as you wish.'

'Thank you.'

The wedding was in the hospital chapel. All the Rinuccis who lived in Naples were there. The women of the family lined up to be the bride's attendants. The men scrapped for the privilege of waiting on Dante.

Toni gave her away, escorting her down the aisle with pride. Dante watched her approach with a look that took her breath away, and that she knew she would remember all her life. As she reached him and laid her hand in his, the problems seemed to melt away. Even the promise he'd imposed on her could not spoil this moment. She was marrying the man she loved, and who loved her. There was nothing else in the world.

Holding Dante's hand in hers, she declared, 'I, Ferne, take you, Dante, to be my husband. I promise to be true to you in good times and in bad, in sickness and in health. I will love you and honour you all the days of my life.'

She knew he wasn't quite ready to understand that. She could only pray for the miracle that would give her the chance to show him.

Then they exchanged rings, the ones that had belonged to his parents, who'd chosen never to be parted. One after the other they recited the ritual wedding-vows, but then the priest looked a silent question, asking if they wished to add anything of their own. Dante nodded, took her hand and spoke in a clear voice for everyone to hear.

'I give you my life for whatever it's worth—not much, perhaps, but there's no part of it that isn't yours. Do with it whatever you will.'

It took her a moment to fight back the tears, but then she said in a shaking voice, 'Everything I am belongs to you. Everything I will ever be belongs to you, now and always—whatever life may bring.'

She said the last words with special significance, hoping he would understand, and she felt him grow still for a moment, looking at her, questioning.

Then it was over. It was time to turn and make their way out of the little chapel, followed by the family.

Instead of a wedding feast they all accompanied Dante to his room, where a smiling nurse showed them in. There was a bottle of champagne to stress that this was a party, but before long the laughter and congratulations faded, as they all remembered why Dante was there.

One by one they bid him goodbye, all of them

knowing that it might be final. Hope and Toni embraced him heartily, then left them alone.

'You must rest well,' the nurse told him. 'So go to bed now, and drink this.' She held up a glass. 'It will help you sleep.'

'I want to stay with him,' Ferne said.

'Of course.'

She helped him undress, and suddenly it was as though a giant machine had taken over. It had started, and nobody could say how it was going to end.

'I'm glad you stayed with me tonight,' he said. 'Because there's still something I need to say to you. I want to ask your forgiveness.'

'For what?'

'For my selfishness. I've had a good look at myself, and I don't like what I see. You were right when you said I shouldn't have let you get so close without telling you the truth.'

'We were supposed to keep it light,' she reminded him.

'But that wasn't under our control. You and I could never have met without loving each other. I loved you from the start, but I wouldn't admit it to myself. Instead I selfishly found excuses, pretending that it wasn't what it was, and I led you into danger.'

'Don't talk of it as danger,' she interrupted him.

'You've been the best experience of my life, and you always will be, whatever happens. Do you understand that? *Whatever happens.*'

'But say you forgive me,' he said. 'I need to hear you say it.' He was already growing sleepy.

'I'll forgive you if you want, but there is nothing to forgive. Please—please try to understand that.'

He smiled but didn't answer. A moment later, his eyes closed. Ferne laid her head down on the pillow beside him, watching him until her own eyes closed.

This was their wedding night.

In the morning the orderlies came to take him to the operating theatre.

'One moment,' Dante said frantically.

As she leaned over him, he touched her face.

'If this should be the last time…' he whispered.

It hit her like a blow. This might really be the last time she touched him, looked into his eyes.

'It isn't the last time,' she said. 'Whatever happens, we will always be together.'

Suddenly he reached out, as though trying to find something.

'What is it?'

'Your camera,' he said. 'The one you always keep with you.'

Now she understood. Pulling it out, she fixed it to take a picture after a few seconds' delay, and set it up a little distance away. Then she took him into her arms, looking into his face.

His own eyes on her were quiet with a peace she had never seen in them before.

'Yes,' he said. 'We'll always be together. I may not be there again, but my love will be, until the end of your life. Tell me that you know that.'

She couldn't speak, only nod.

Then it was time. The orderlies wheeled him away. Suddenly it was all over; she might never see him alive again.

'Suppose he dies?' she said to Hope, distraught. 'Dies in an operation that he only had because I made him? He might have lived for years without getting sick. If he dies, I'll have killed him.'

'And if it goes well, you will have saved his life and his sanity,' Hope said firmly.

How slowly the hours passed. Many times she took out the camera and studied the last picture she'd taken. It was tiny, but she could see Dante's face turned towards her with an expression of adoration that startled her. Had it been there before, and had she just never noticed? Would it be the last of him that she ever saw?

What had she done to him?

She seemed to see her life stretching before

her, with an empty place where he should have been. There was her child, asking where her father was, and not understanding that her mother had sent him to his death.

The years would pass and their child would grow, become a success, married. But without a father to show his pride and love.

'I took it away from him,' she mourned.

'No,' Hope said. 'You have to understand that Dante was right about doing the quick-step with fate. He's giving himself the best chance, or rather, you've given it to him. You were fate's instrument. Now it's out of our hands.'

At last he was wheeled out of the operating theatre, his head swathed in bandages. He looked pale, ghostly, and completely unlike the Dante they knew. But he was alive.

'It went well,' the doctor told them. 'He's strong, and there were no complications, so we were able to support the wall of the weak artery with less difficulty than usual. It's too soon for certainty, but I expect him to live.'

'And—the other thing?' Ferne stammered.

'That we'll have to wait and see. It's a pity he delayed treatment for so long, but I'm hopeful.'

That qualification haunted her as she sat beside Dante's bed, waiting for him to awaken. She didn't know how long she was there. It was a long time since she'd slept, but however weary she was she knew she couldn't sleep now.

Hour after hour passed. He lay terrifyingly still, attached to so many machines that he almost disappeared under them. Part of his face was invisible beneath the huge plug clamping his mouth and attaching him to the breathing machine.

She had seen him wicked, charming, cruel, but never until this moment had she seen him totally helpless.

Perhaps it was for ever. Perhaps she had condemned him to this, although he'd begged her not to. He'd asked her forgiveness, but now, in the long dark hours, she fervently asked for his.

'I may have taken everything away from you,' she whispered. 'You tried to warn me, but now, if your life is ruined, it's my fault. Forgive me. Forgive me.'

He lay motionless and silent. The only sound in the room was the machine helping him to breathe.

Dawn broke, and she realised that she'd been there all night. A doctor came to detach the breathing machine, saying, 'Let's see how well he manages without it.'

Ferne stood well back while the plug was removed from his mouth and the machine pulled away. There was a pause, while time seemed to stop, then Dante gave a small choke and drew in a long breath.

'Excellent,' the doctor declared. 'Breathing normal.'

'How long before he comes round?' Ferne asked.

'He needs a bit longer.'

He departed and she settled back beside the bed, taking Dante's hand in hers.

'You've made a great start,' she told him.

Could he hear her? she wondered. Hearing was supposed to outlast all the other senses. Perhaps if she could reach him now she could even help to keep his brain strong.

'It's going to be all right,' she said, leaning close. 'You're going to wake up and be just the same as I've always known you—scheming, manipulative, dodgy, a man to be avoided by a woman with any sense. But I've never had any sense where you were concerned. I should have given in the first day, shouldn't I? Except that I think I did, and much good it did me. Do you remember?'

He lay still, giving no sign of hearing.

She went on talking, not knowing what she said or how much time passed. The words didn't matter. Most of them were nonsense, the kind of nonsense they had always talked—but he must surely hear the underlying message, which was an impassioned plea to him to return to her.

'Don't leave me alone without you; come back to me.'

But he lay so still that he might already have gone into another world. At last, leaning down, she kissed him softly on the lips.

'I love you,' she whispered at last. 'That's all there is to say.'

Then she jerked back, startled. Had he moved?

She watched closely. It was true; he moved.

A sigh broke from him, and he murmured something.

'What did you say?' she asked. 'Speak to me.'

'Portia,' he whispered.

'What was that?'

After a moment, he repeated the word. 'Portia—I'm so glad you're here.'

She wanted to cry aloud in her despair. He didn't know her. His brain was failing, as he'd feared. Whoever Portia was, she was there inside with him.

Slowly he opened his eyes.

'Hello,' he murmured. 'Why are you crying?'

'I'm not—I was just happy to have you back.'

He gave a sleepy smile. 'You were calling me names—scheming, manipulative, dodgy. Never mind. My little friend will stand up for me.'

'Your little friend?' she asked, scarcely daring to breathe.

'Our daughter. I've been getting to know her. I

want to call her Portia. She likes it. Darling Ferne, don't cry. Everything's going to be all right.'

It took time to believe that his recovery was complete, for the news seemed too good to be true. But with every hour that passed Dante showed that his faculties were as sharp as ever.

'We played fate at his own game,' he told her. 'And we won. Or, rather, you did. You were the player. Before you came, I never had the nerve to take that game on. Without you, I should never have had it.'

He touched her face.

'I see you there so clearly, and everything around you; all the world is clear. I hadn't dared to dream that this would happen.'

'It's what I always believed,' she said.

'I know, but I couldn't be sure. There was always the chance that you might have had to put me in an institution.'

Ferne hesitated. It would have been so easy to let this moment slip past and be forgotten, but something impelled her to total honesty, whatever the risk.

'Oh no,' she said. 'I would never have done that.'

He frowned. 'But you promised, don't you remember?'

'I know what I promised,' she said calmly. 'But

nothing would have made me keep that promise. Even now I don't think you begin to understand how much I love you. Whatever happened, I would have kept you with me. If you were ill, that would have been more reason to love you, but you were in no state to understand it then. So I had to practise a little deception.'

He looked stunned, as though the full power of her declaration was only just dawning on him.

'But,' he whispered at last, 'you promised on everything you hold dear and sacred.'

'I lied,' she said calmly. 'You wanted to be kept out of sight, so that's what I would have done— but you would have been in our home, where the world couldn't see you, but I could see you every day. Whether you were yourself, or whether your mind had gone, you would have been my husband and I would have loved you until the last moment of my life.'

Suddenly, shockingly, she found her temper rising. Why should she have to explain all this to him?

'So now you know,' she said. 'I lied to you. I wanted to marry you so much, I'd have said and done anything. I made that promise without the most distant intention of keeping it, because I loved you with all of my heart and all of my *life*— but you just couldn't realise, could you?

'Can you see it now? Or are you just too proud and arrogant—and too *stupid*—to understand? You think love is a matter of making bargains, and you can't get it into your head that love has to be unconditional. If it isn't unconditional, it isn't love.'

She waited to see if he would say anything, but he seemed too stunned to speak. Was she being foolish? she wondered. Was she risking their marriage for the satisfaction of getting this off her chest?

But she had no choice. If they were to stand a chance, the air must be clear between them.

'So now you know the worst about me,' she said. 'I tricked you into marriage by deceit. I'm a shameless, dishonest woman who'll do anything to get her own way.'

When at last Dante spoke, he said only two words, and they were the last words Ferne expected to hear.

'Thank goodness!'

'What was that?'

'Thank goodness you're a liar, my darling! Thank goodness you had the courage to be shameless and deceitful. When I think of the disaster that could have befallen me if you'd been truthful, I tremble inside.'

'What—what are you talking about?' she said, half-laughing, half-afraid to believe her ears.

'I never felt I had the right to marry you, knowing what I might be leading you into. It was my way of setting you free. If you'd refused to promise, I'd have forced myself to refuse the marriage, although to be your husband was what I wanted with all my heart. In life, in death, or in that half-life I dreaded so much, I want you, and only you, to be there with me.

'But that felt like selfishness. I demanded that promise because I believed I had no right to trap you and blight your life.'

'But you could never blight my life,' she protested. 'You *are* my life. Haven't you understood that?'

'I guess I'm just starting to. It seemed too much to hope that you should love me as much as I love you. I still can't quite take it in, but I know this: my life belongs to you. Not only because we married, but because the life I have now is the life you gave me.

'Take it, and use it as you will. It was you who drove the clouds away, and you who brings the sunlight. And, as long as you are with me, that will always be true.'

Two weeks later Dante was discharged from hospital, and he and Ferne went to spend a few weeks at the Villa Rinucci. Even when they returned to their apartment they lived quietly, the only excitement being the delayed wedding-breakfast, celebrated when the whole Rinucci family was present.

After that everyone held their breath for the birth of the newest family member. Portia Rinucci was born the next spring, a combination of her mother's looks and her father's spirit. At her christening, it was observed by everyone that it was her father who held her possessively, his face blazing with love and pride, while her mother looked on with fond tolerance, perfectly happy with the unusual arrangement.

If sometimes Ferne's eyes darkened, it was only because she could never quite forget the cloud that had retreated but not completely vanished. As her daughter grew, it might yet darken their lives again—but she would face it, strengthened by a triumphant love and a happiness that few women knew.

* * * * *

Rancher Ramsey Westmoreland's temporary cook is way too attractive for his liking. Little does he know Chloe Burton came to his ranch with another agenda entirely....

That man across the street had to be, without a doubt, the most handsome man she'd ever seen.

Chloe Burton's pulse beat rhythmically as he stopped to talk to another man in front of a feed store. He was tall, dark and every inch of sexy—from his Stetson to the well-worn leather boots on his feet. And from the way his jeans and Western shirt fit his broad muscular shoulders, it was quite obvious he had everything it took to separate the men from the boys. The combination was enough to corrupt any woman's mind and had her weakening even from a distance. Her body felt flushed. It was hot. Unsettled.

Over the past year the only male who had gotten her time and attention had been the e-mail. That was simply pathetic, especially since now she was practically drooling simply at the sight of a man. Even his stance—both hands in his jeans pockets, legs braced apart, was a pose she would carry to her dreams.

And he was smiling, evidently enjoying the conversation being exchanged. He had dimples, incredibly sexy dimples in not one but both cheeks.

"What are you staring at, Clo?"

Chloe nearly jumped. She'd forgotten she had a lunch date. She glanced over the table at her best friend from college, Lucia Conyers.

"Take a look at that man across the street in the blue shirt, Lucia. Will he not be perfect for Denver's first issue of *Simply Irresistible* or what?" Chloe asked with so much excitement she almost couldn't stand it.

She was the owner of *Simply Irresistible*, a magazine for today's up-and-coming woman. Their once-a-year Irresistible Man cover, which highlighted a man the magazine felt deserved the honor, had increased sales enough for Chloe to open a Denver office.

When Lucia didn't say anything but kept staring, Chloe's smile widened. "Well?"

Lucia glanced across the booth at her. "Since you asked, I'll tell you what I see. One of the Westmorelands—Ramsey Westmoreland. And yes, he'd be perfect for the cover, but he won't do it."

Chloe raised a brow. "He'd get paid for his services, of course."

Lucia laughed and shook her head. "Getting paid won't be the issue, Clo—Ramsey is one of the wealthiest sheep ranchers in this part of

Colorado. But everyone knows what a private person he is. Trust me—he won't do it."

Chloe couldn't help but smile. The man was the epitome of what she was looking for in a magazine cover and she was determined that whatever it took, he would be it.

"Umm, I don't like that look on your face, Chloe. I've seen it before and know exactly what it means."

She watched as Ramsey Westmoreland entered the store with a swagger that made her almost breathless. She *would* be seeing him again.

Look for Silhouette Desire's
HOT WESTMORELAND NIGHTS
by Brenda Jackson,
available March 9 wherever books are sold.

Dear Reader,

When I started writing the first book in my Rinucci series, five years ago, I had no idea what an enjoyable task it was going to be. But as the work developed I discovered that the real joy was not just six attractive heroes, but the feeling of being drawn into a large, united family, where people will do anything for each other. As Dante Rinucci says, "There's nothing to compare with the feeling that you have the whole tribe behind you."

So when it came to writing a seventh Rinucci book I was really glad to go back to the Villa Rinucci in Naples and meet all my old friends again.

Dante is a cousin, not a brother, but since his parents died he has lived part of the time at the villa, and has come to see Hope and Toni as extra parents. He's a man practiced in keeping secrets, since beneath the laughing exterior he's concealing the tragic knowledge that he might be suffering from an inherited ailment that could lie dormant for years, then suddenly end his life or render him mentally disabled. Of the two, it's the second one he fears.

To cope, he lives for the moment, avoiding long-term commitments, until he meets the one woman he can love deeply enough to risk the future, and whose own love is deep enough to take the risk with him.

So here's the seventh Rinucci, as crazy, charming and infuriating—but also as passionately loving—as the others.

Warmest wishes,

Lucy Gordon

INTERNATIONAL GROOMS

Choose your dream destination to say "I Do"!

Applegate Ranch, Montana:
Get your lasso at the ready for rugged rancher Dillon in
RODEO BRIDE by Myrna Mackenzie

Loire Valley, France:
You don't need a magic wand for a fairy tale in France,
with handsome château owner Alex as your host!
CINDERELLA ON HIS DOORSTEP
by Rebecca Winters

Principality of Carvainia, Mediterranean:
Step into Aleks's turreted castle
and you'll feel like a princess!
HER PRINCE'S SECRET SON
by Linda Goodnight

Manhattan, New York:
Stroll down Fifth Avenue
on the arm of self-made millionaire Houston.
RESCUED IN A WEDDING DRESS
by Cara Colter

Naples, Italy:
The majesty of Mount Vesuvius and dangerously
dashing Dante will make your senses erupt!
ACCIDENTALLY EXPECTING!
by Lucy Gordon

Sydney, Australia:
Hotshot TV producer Dan is on the lookout
for someone to star in his life....
LIGHTS, CAMERA...KISS THE BOSS
by Nikki Logan